HOUND
HEAVEN

HOUND
HEAVEN

Linda Oatman High

Boyds Mills Press

Library of Congress Cataloging-in-Publication Data
High, Linda Oatman.
Hound heaven / Linda Oatman High.—1st ed.
184 p.   cm.
Originally published: N.Y.: Holiday House, 1995.
Summary. Living with her grandfather on Muckwater Mountain in
West Virginia, twelve-year-old Silver aggressively pursues her dream of
having a dog by working to earn the money for one.
ISBN 1-59078-244-5
[1. Grandfathers—Fiction.   2. Mountain lfe—West Virginia—Fiction.
3. West Virginia—Fiction.   4. Dogs—Fiction.   5. Moneymaking
projects—Fiction.]   I. Title.
pZ7.H543968Ho   1995   2003112910   CIP   AC
[Fic]—dc20

Published by Boyds Mills Press, Inc.
A Highlights Company
815 Church Street
Honesdale, Pennsylvania 18431

Printed in China
Visit our Web site at www.boydsmillspress.com
First Boyds Mills Press paperback edition, 2004
10 9 8 7 6 5 4 3 2 1

For John, whose faith in me and my dreams is as a million grains of mustard seed, making nothing impossible.

With thanks to:

My son, Justin, for the seed of an idea found in his stack of newspaper dogs.

Pat Silvers, for introducing me to Delilah, a greyhound dog with the soul of an angel.

My mom and dad, for allowing me to pluck my dream dog from the snow and keep her forever, making my Hound Heaven come true.

And Margery Cuyler, for making things truly heavenlike happen with her editorial wisdom and spiritual vision.

CONTENTS

HOUND
HEAVEN

1

Fifty-Two Dogs
Stuck on the Ceiling

IT WAS DARKER THAN THE DARK between the stars, and I lay flat on my back in bed . . . waiting.

Sure enough, it started: Papaw's snoring, snuffling and snarkling, and sawing logs, with a cuss word cutting in every now and then. Even in sleep, Papaw was about as uncultivated as the overgrown garden weeding through the woods behind our tar paper shack.

I clicked on Papaw's old flashlight and beamed it at the ceiling above my bed. Sliding the circle of brightness slowly back and forth, up and down and all around, I shed light on each dog.

There were Cleopatra and Johann Sebastian Bach and Elvis. There were Herbert Hoover and

Harry Houdini and Hemingway. There were Plato and Pearly, Sparkles and Spot, King and Queen, and Princess and Prince.

There were fifty-two dogs stuck on the ceiling, a year's worth of clippings from the *Sunday News*. Papaw called my collection Hound Heaven. I called it my Dream Dog Display.

Every Sunday, right after church, I grabbed the local section of the *Swampville Sunday News* and opened straight to the Humane League adoption column. It was a ritual, an end-of-the-week routine that annoyed Papaw to no end.

"Don't know why you waste your time," he grexed as I carefully clipped the column at the kitchen table. "You'll get a dog over my dead body."

I hated when he said that. The word *dead* was one that I steered clear of, ever since Mama and Daddy and my baby sister Emmie lit off for Heaven and left me stranded with Papaw on Muckwater Mountain, in this two-room shack of tar paper and log. Bark Shanty, as Papaw proclaimed with his hand-carved wooden sign creaking out front by the road. You'd think it was an estate or something, the way Papaw bragged on the place.

"It's not fancy, but it's clean," he always said.

"And paid for." Then he'd ramble on about how he and Mamaw built Bark Shanty with their very own hands and cleared the land and planted the garden, raising my mama there and growing old together. And now look: Mamaw was gone, so was Mama, Bark Shanty was falling apart, the garden was a mess of weeds and poison ivy, and the land (two acres and a quarter, according to Papaw) was a swamp crawling with snakes and skunkweed. Some estate.

"Silver," Papaw said, spitting out my name the same way he spewed his chew, "you should be grateful for what you've got."

And I was, I reckon. At least I had a roof over my head and a bed to sleep in and food on the table. But I didn't have a lot of clothes or a canopy bed or dreamcatcher earrings like my best friend, Rose. I didn't have a mama or a daddy or a baby sister anymore. I didn't have a boyfriend. And I didn't have a dog. There were lots of things I didn't have.

"No room in Bark Shanty for a dog," Papaw said. "Why, there's barely enough room for an old man and a twelve-year-old girl."

"Almost thirteen," I reminded him. What I didn't tell Papaw was that I was bound and determined to have a dog by the time my birthday rolled around at the tail end of July. It was now April, so that gave me almost four months to talk sense into Papaw.

"Why do you want a dog so bad, Silver?" asked Rose, her dreamcatchers swinging in the sunlight. Rose swore up and down that those earrings filtered out her dreams, catching the good and letting the bad run on through. To me, they looked like circles of spider webs with a hunk of turquoise stone stuck smack-dab in the middle, dangling and tangling in her long red hair. To Rose, they were magic.

"I want a dog," I said, feeling the old familiar ache deep inside, "so that I have somebody to love."

Rose laughed. "A *dog* isn't a *somebody*," she said. "It's just a *dog*."

I sighed. Rose didn't understand. Nobody did. There was not a living soul on this earth who knew how empty I was in that place where my heart used to be, back in the days before Mama and Daddy and Emmie were killed in the car crash. I was in school, in *science class* no less, when it happened. I hated science class.

I tried hard to explain it to Rose, figuring that if anybody would understand, it would be her.

"There's nothing here anymore, Rose," I said, thumping my chest.

"There never was," she replied, smiling. "That's why you wear training bras with little blue flowers in the middle."

"Rose," I said, not telling her that I snipped off all those blue flowers after she told me they showed plain as day through my clothes, "I'm empty. It's as if my heart is shattered into a million pieces and scattered all through my body, poking holes here and there and letting everything good leak out."

Rose just looked confounded, so I went on. "I'm lonely," I said. "I'm as alone as a scarecrow."

I stopped talking and took a deep breath, letting my words settle. Rose looked at me, her eyes tiny blue pinpricks of squint behind her pink-rimmed glasses.

"And you think a *dog* can fix all that?" she asked.

So I gave up. The innards of Silver Iris Nickles couldn't be brought out with all the words in West Virginia. I couldn't explain the hurt inside of me, any more than I could explain why the sky was blue or the sun was yellow. Even Rose, who would have been my bosom buddy if I *had* a bosom, just didn't get it.

The only time I felt anywhere near half happy was when I lay in bed at night, listening to Papaw's snores and gazing up at my Dream Dogs. I always waited for Papaw to fall asleep so that he wouldn't fuss about his flashlight batteries. And then I'd just gawk at those dogs to my heart's content, reciting their names like Bible verses.

That's what I was doing on that dark night in April, a night blacker than tar.

"Rufus and Rex and Romeo," I whispered, holding the flashlight like a holy white candle in my hands. "Sargent and Sancho and Snowy." Then I finished, as always, like a prayer. Only I didn't say A-men. I said *A-dog*.

And on that night, that tar-dark night, I did something different. I changed my prayer, the one Mama taught me when I was little.

Mama's version—the one I said every night—went like this: "Now I lay me down to sleep, I pray the Lord my soul to keep. Thy love go with me through the night, and wake me with the morning light."

It was crazy, but I looked up at that collection of gray newspaper dogs, and a new prayer came pouring out of me like Puppy Chow.

"Now I lay me down to sleep, I'd really love

a dog a heap. And if You send it by July, I'll bake you, Lord, a rhubarb pie. I smiled and clicked off the flashlight, stashing it beneath my pillow. "A-men," I whispered, closing my eyes and seeing Mama and Daddy and Emmie flying across the back of my eyelids with wings of shimmering gold, toting chunks of my broken heart as they flew.

I started, jerking, and opened my eyes. And then I saw it, shining through the stained-glass window Papaw had made for my room. It was the moon, moving from behind a cloud like a gliding Frisbee. It slid smoothly across the glass, stopping directly in the middle of the window, so that my Dream Dogs were illuminated in shades of soft red and purple and green. It was the brightest and whitest moon I ever saw in all my days, and the biggest. And then, clear as the nose on my face, it winked. The man in the moon, or whatever it was, winked at *me:* Silver Iris Nickles.

That was the moment I knew, pure and true, that something heavenlike was bound to happen.

Easter Blind Bunny

It was the eve of Easter, and we were painting Papaw's toenails. Pale pink, kind of a coral seashell shade that Rose found in her mama's makeup bag.

"Sshhh," I hissed, laughing harder than I'd laughed in a long time.

"What are you worried about, Silver?" Rose asked, snickering as she stroked polish across Papaw's big, jagged-edged toenail. "You said he sleeps as heavy as undercooked dumplings."

"Oh," I said, waving my hand above Papaw's foot to dry the polish. "That reminds me. I made up this new prayer about how I want a dog. And guess what I promised the Lord if He sends one to me?"

Rose shrugged, twisting the cap onto the

bottle of pink polish and sticking it in her pocket. Prayers and the Lord were two subjects Rose shied away from, same way she avoided church on Sunday morning. Rose Roberts didn't put much stock into things of a spiritual nature, only material things. Rose liked things she could see and smell and touch, things like jewelry and perfume and silky, swishy skirts that showed off her legs. To Rose, the Lord was just another fairy tale and talking to Him was akin to having a conversation with an elf. I knew full well that Rose thought I was nuts for praying every night, but I didn't care. I *needed* to pray, to believe that a power greater than me was in control, because I sure wasn't. I no more had control of my life than Papaw had control of his snores, which were exploding from his throat as if he'd swallowed every spring frog in the swamp.

"I promised the Lord," I said, talking over Papaw's racket, "that if He sends me a dog, I'll bake Him a rhubarb pie." I grinned.

"Silver!" Rose squealed, and Papaw stirred, groaning. Rose slapped her hand over her mouth, and I switched off Papaw's light, leading Rose into my room. As there were only two rooms in the place, we referred to them as my room and Papaw's room. My room was smaller, but nicer, with the stained-glass window and the little rolltop desk and Mamaw's antique wardrobe in the corner. Papaw's room served as kitchen, living room, bathroom (there was a claw-foot tub behind a curtain, beside the woodstove), and workroom for his stained-glass business. Papaw slept on the sofa, ever since I barged in on him a year ago.

"Silver," Rose said, flopping onto my bed, "you're insane. Why would the Lord, if there really is one, need a rhubarb pie? I'm sure there's plenty to eat up there at that big church picnic in the sky." She said this in the voice she used when she was being sarcastic, as Rose didn't believe in Heaven any more than she believed in Santa Claus.

"It's not for Him to eat," I said, sitting at the desk. "Of course the Lord doesn't need a rhubarb pie. But what He does need is to see that I'm doing something I truly hate, just for Him. And you know how I hate to bake."

Rose giggled, tossing my musical dog, Woof-Woof, into the air. Woof-Woof was a windup dog that tinkled out the tune "That Doggie in the Window." Mama and Daddy gave him to me when I turned two, and I gave him his name. He used to wag his tail and pant, too, but now his tongue and tail were both broken off.

"Oh, Lord," Rose intoned, flinging Woof-Woof high above the bed and catching him in her arms, "please send a doggie flying from Heaven for Silver Nickles. Please, pretty please, with a cherry on top and a slab of homemade whipped cream on rhubarb pie. Mail a mutt, express delivery from the church picnic in the sky. Silver Nickles wants puppy love. She wants to smooch a pooch." Rose loudly smacked Woof-Woof's face and then kissed him all over his matted fur.

"Rose," I said, not laughing. "Your sense of humor is really warped sometimes."

Rose leaped up from the bed and sashayed to the window, hugging Woof-Woof. "How much is that doggie in the window," she sang, holding Woof-Woof in front of the stained glass, "the one with the broken-off tail." She swayed Woof-Woof to the tune, and I had to laugh, despite myself.

"You're weird, Rose Roberts," I said.

"*Me!*" Rose said, tossing the dog onto the bed. "*You're* the one who came up with the idea of painting your papaw's toenails while he sleeps."

"Oh," I said, remembering something. "I

need to write that letter." I opened the desk, pulling out a piece of yellow paper.

"Dear Mr. Bills," I scrawled. "Please forgive me for accidentally painting your toenails last night. You see, I'm a very old rabbit, and my eyesight isn't so good. I'm sure *you* understand, Mr. Bills, as I noticed your glasses on the table. I tried wearing them, but that made my problem even worse, and I ended up coloring your toenails rather than the eggs. This is a problem that has happened in the past and most certainly will happen again, if we're not careful. But I do have a suggestion to avoid this from happening in the future. My advice is to get a dog who will help to guide me through the night and find the eggs. Any dog will do, but he must like rabbits. I have never made this mistake in a home with a dog. At least *your* toenails are all pale pink, Mr. Bills. You should have seen this one old geezer with a different color on each toe, and his fingernails, too! Hope it never happens to *you*. Well, I must hop off across the mountain now. Tell your granddaughter thank you for the lettuce and carrots. Hope you like your candy and that you don't wear open-toed shoes for the Easter egg hunt! You'd be the talk of Muckwater

Mountain. Hippity, hippity, hop . . . hey! See you next year . . . Easter B. Bunny."

Rose laughed, reading over my shoulder. "He's going to kill you, Silver. What does the 'B' stand for, anyway?"

I grinned. "Blind," I said. "Easter Blind Bunny."

Rose shook her head, jabbing at her glasses. "He's going to kill you," she said again.

I folded the paper and tiptoed to the kitchen table, where our Easter baskets sat waiting. Last year, on my first Easter with Papaw, he forgot all about candy and eggs and baskets and such. So this year, I'd taken it upon myself to go shopping with Rose's family, using the money I earned selling swamp frogs to the Muckwater Critters Pet Store. I bought baskets—purple for Papaw and pink for me—and plastic eggs in every color of the rainbow. I bought yellow marshmallow chicks and blue-speckled robin's eggs and malted-milk balls. I bought a box of those fancy once-a-year Cadbury eggs with the cream and the yolk, and I bought a hog's mess of peanut-butter eggs, Papaw's favorite. I even bought two chocolate bunny rabbits with hard-candy eyes and molded flowers, which cost me an arm and a leg. But it was *Easter*, and Easter was supposed to be special. So I made it special.

I folded the note and stuck it in Papaw's basket, right between the bunny rabbit and a Cadbury egg. Papaw snorted, and I jumped, thinking of the conniption fit he'd throw in the morning when he looked down and saw ten pink piggies peeking up at him. I snickered and tiptoed back into my room.

"He's going to kill you," Rose said again.

"Oh, well," I said, shrugging. "At least then I'd join Mama and Daddy and Emmie."

Rose rolled her eyes and shook her head, her shiny red hair falling across her shoulders. "You believe in everything," she said. "Love and faith and hope and Heaven and hound dogs and talking to somebody you can't even see." She yanked on her jacket, which was as clean and white as new snow.

"And you," I said, "don't believe in anything. Except maybe makeup and dreamcatchers and magic." I opened the door of Mamaw's old wardrobe and peered into the wrinkled wavy mirror hanging inside.

"Just look," I said, "at how different we are." Rose came and stood beside me. "You have red hair; I have dirty-dishwater hair. You have curves; I'm as skinny as a pole. You have blue eyes; mine are as brown as mud. You're beautiful; I'm not." I slammed shut the door.

"You are plumb crazy, Silver Nickles," Rose said, heading for the door. She looked up at my Dream Dog Display. "And you might as well rip those mongrels off your ceiling, because I'll tell you one thing I know for sure."

"What?" I asked, flopping down on the bed.

"You'll have a boyfriend before you have a dog," said Rose. "So you'd best get to work cutting boys from your yearbook and pasting *them* all over the place." She smiled and went out the door, disappearing like melted chocolate into the night.

"You're wrong, Rose Roberts," I said, flicking off the light and flooding my room with darkness. "You're *dead* wrong."

It was the first time I'd said the word in more than a year.

Papaw's Pink Toenails

"WHAT IN TARNATION . . . " Papaw's voice rumbled like thunder into my dream.

I rolled over and stretched, smiling, and then climbed out of bed and headed for Papaw's room.

"What's wrong, Papaw?" I asked, biting the insides of my mouth to keep from smiling. "Didn't you get any peanut-butter eggs?"

Papaw was standing by the sofa in his rumpled old green-and-white flannel pajamas, looking down at his feet. Actually, he was *staring* down at his feet, gawking as if he'd seen a ghost skim across his toes. "Silver Iris Nickles," he said, lifting his face to stare at me.

I looked straight back at him, thinking how his face was looking older every day. Papaw had a face like a mountain rock, all hard with cracks and lines in it. I remember when I was about five, before Mamaw died, I told Papaw that his face looked like Mamaw's wrinkled old leather pocketbook. He was that old, even back then.

Papaw stood as still as stone, staring away with this befuddled look in his eyes. Papaw's eyes were brown, like mine and Mama's, and his lips were all puckered together without his dentures. "Silver Iris Nickles," he said again, and I knew then I was really in trouble. Papaw never said my full name twice in one day.

"What?" I asked, as calm as milk. Even though Papaw was mad as a wet hen, I knew he'd never hurt me. Papaw looked mean, but in reality he was harmless as the Avon lady.

"You know what," Papaw said and pointed down at his toes. I moved closer and looked, all curiouslike.

"Oh, my heavens!" I said, smacking my hand across my mouth. "Your toenails are pink, Papaw. Reckon you finally broke down and bought something from that Avon lady?"

"Silver Iris Nickles," Papaw said, and my name sounded like cusswords. I looked down again, and his toenails seemed to be smiling up at me, all perky and bright and cheery. I couldn't help but chuckle, seeing those ten pink spots topping off Papaw's big, bony feet.

"Let's go see what the Easter Bunny left in our baskets, Papaw," I said. "It's almost time for church."

Papaw obeyed me like a little kid, shuffling across the linoleum in his pajamas. He put on his glasses and peered into his basket and then gazed down at his feet. "Even worse than I thought," he muttered.

"What's that paper, Papaw?" I pointed to the yellow sheet, waving like a flag behind the bunny.

Papaw looked at me and pulled the letter from the basket. He read it, his lips moving, and then stuck it back in place. "You'll get a dog over my dead body, Silver," he said, plucking an egg from the bottom of the basket.

I went cold all over, hearing those words again. "I wish you wouldn't say that," I said. "I really wish you wouldn't."

"I wish lots of things," Papaw said, "but they never come true. Wishes and prayers, they don't change things a bit." He reached for the cup that held his teeth, swishing them around in the liquid. "If wishes and prayers did any good," he said, popping his choppers into his mouth, "your mama and your mamaw would both be here today, eating chocolate and going to church like nobody's business."

I took a deep breath, feeling the tears welling up inside. Papaw hardly ever talked about Mama or Mamaw, and when he did, we both usually ended up crying.

Papaw turned his back to me, hobbling over to the coffeepot, and suddenly I wanted to bawl at the thought of those polished toenails. Mama always polished her toenails, and her fingernails, and her soul. Mama had the shiniest soul of anybody I ever knew. I could just imagine her now: the most shimmery angel in Heaven, except for maybe baby Emmie.

I watched Papaw brew coffee, his fuzzy tufts of star-white hair downy as dandelion fluff above his tired eyes. I watched him as he watched the coffee, feeling sad at the sight of those eyes so like mine. Mud brown, with light yellow pinwheels when you looked real close. Mama used to say that our eyes were like sunshine on swamp soil. I believe that Emmie's eyes would have been like that, if she'd lived long enough to cry all the blue out of them. My eyes were blue, too, until I was seven months old.

I sat at the table, in my rickety old high-backed

chair, and traced daisies on the oilcloth. Papaw sat down across from me, slurping his coffee.

"Are you going to church today, Papaw?" I asked, tracing the petals of a daisy. *He loves me, he loves me not.* Rose always did that with the petals, tossing them into the wind as if she couldn't care less if she was loved or not. I always figured that was because Rose knew full well that she *was* loved, what with that canopy bed and all.

"Nah," Papaw said. "Don't go to church any other Sunday."

"But it's Easter," I said.

Papaw shrugged, his bony shoulders jutting up toward his ears. "Every day is something," he said.

I sighed, standing and glancing at the cat-shaped clock ticking its tail over the icebox. Mamaw had loved cats. "Time for me to get ready," I said, heading for my room.

I padded past the baskets, snitching the yellow note on my way. "Rubbing alcohol will take that paint off your toes," I said quietly, not turning to look at Papaw.

And then I went into my room and tore the note up into a zillion pieces.

Faith and a Mustard Seed

From MY SEAT IN THE BACK PEW, I thought that the church looked more like a flower garden than the Muckwater Mountain Tabernacle of God. There were flowers on hats, flowers on dresses, flowers in hair, flowers on jackets. I wondered what it was about Easter morning that made folks so downright flowery.

I was wearing a plain green dress that Mama made for me when I was eleven. It had hitched higher up my legs in the last year, but the styles were shorter this spring, according to Rose. So I reckon I must have been the height of high fashion, what with my skimpy green dress and the mustard-seed necklace dangling down my chest.

I found the necklace tucked away in the

corner of Mamaw's wardrobe, right after I moved in with Papaw. It was a chain of looped golden links, with a plastic dome hanging from it. Within the dome was a tiny kernel of something that rolled and rattled when you shook it.

"Look, Papaw," I said, draping the chain around my neck.

Papaw's eyes clouded, and he gently fastened the clasp beneath my hair. "This was your mama's," he said. "Her mustard-seed necklace."

"Mustard seed?" I asked, jiggling the dome.

Papaw nodded. "She got it for perfect attendance at Sunday school when she was about your age," he said. "Came with that Bible verse tucked inside, the one about having faith even as a grain of mustard seed."

"Where's the verse?" I asked, peering inside the cloudy plastic.

"Must have been lost somewhere along the way," Papaw said. "Just like my faith."

Sitting in church on Easter morning, I slowly rattled the mustard seed and thought about faith. There was a poster in the school library that said: "The reason birds can fly and we can't is simply that they have perfect faith, for to have faith is to have wings." I'd memorized that poster, thinking of Mama's faith and how she was flying high in Heaven because of it. There was a picture of a little white bird soaring through the sky, which always made me think of Emmie. If Mama's soul was polished and shiny, Emmie's was white and tiny and pure. Daddy's was slightly gray, on account of his smoking and drinking and all, but I knew without a doubt that his soul was up there gallivanting through Heaven with Mama and Emmie. It made me a tad bit jealous, thinking of the three of them up there and me down here.

Pastor Pete was saying something about faith, and I let go of my necklace, letting it hang heavy and still beneath my heart. "We walk by faith, not by sight," he said.

I started to giggle, thinking of Easter Blind Bunny's poor sight. That rabbit must have been walking by lots of faith, to have the gall to paint Walter Bills's toenails. Coral pink, no less. I bit my lip, thinking of Papaw smearing away at the paint with a cotton ball full of rubbing alcohol.

And then Pastor Pete said something that popped out at me like a jack-in-the-box. "Faith without works is dead," he said.

Sitting there alone in the back pew, I suddenly knew what I had to do if my dream dog was to become a reality. I had to *work*, doggone it. Faith and wishes and prayers and my Dream Dog Display were all well and good, but those things alone wouldn't bring me my dog. Pink polish on Papaw's toenails and a note from the Easter Bunny wouldn't make a puppy magically materialize before my eyes. I had to *work*. The idea rose within me like a sunrise, and I smiled, thinking of how I'd earn the money for rawhide chews and puppy food and a sturdy red leash. I'd buy one of those fancy doghouses shaped like a castle, and a big blue bowl. A collar with a bell and a soft, plushy doggie bed, all done up in cushions of foam. I'd get some of that high-priced dog shampoo to make the mutt smell like a springtime flower garden, and powder to scare off the ticks and fleas. I'd get a brush and a ball and a big bone of rubber. Shoot, I'd even give a donation to the Humane League, just like putting money in the collection plate at church. Papaw would soften up for sure, seeing the fruits of my labor. He always was one to believe in the value of hard work.

I looked through the church window, seeing a bit of our yard and a little chunk of the shack. The Tabernacle of God and Bark Shanty faced each other kind of cockeyed across Boghill

Road, and from the back pew I could catch a view of my bedroom window. I always thought it was so strange, the way my Bark Shanty bedroom was done up in stained glass while the Tabernacle of God had plain old windows. Papaw said he once asked Pastor Pete if the church wanted some stained glass to liven up the place.

"No, thank you, Brother Walt," said Pastor Pete. "We like to look out at the world so's we can see who needs saving." Papaw took that as an insult, seeing as how Bark Shanty was the only other building in sight.

And now, as I watched through the window, Papaw hobbled out into the yard. He hated how he couldn't move anywhere near as fast as in his younger days. Blamed it on that sliver of shrapnel in his knee, which had been there since whatever war it was Papaw had fought. Sometimes I felt that he and I were at war, every day.

Papaw limped out toward the outhouse, the straps of his bib overalls flapping. I glanced around the church, hoping that nobody else was looking. Nobody was, so I slowly turned my head to the window again.

What I saw made me sit up straight in my

seat on that Sunday morning. A boy—a strange boy I'd never laid eyes on before—was sneaking up behind Papaw with something shiny in his hand.

5

The Dud at the Outhouse

IT WAS A LEASH, a sparkly leash studded with golden rhinestones. And on the end of that leash was the prissiest little pooch I ever saw, a tiny black poodle with her ears all done up in bows of lavender velvet.

On the *other* end of that glittery leash was a boy so scrawny and pale that he looked like death warmed over. The boy was about as tall as I was, with dark-rimmed glasses and greasy black hair that spilled like oil across his forehead.

"Down yonder," Papaw was saying as I walked across Boghill Road, "the way the crow flies, about a mile." His overalls were still unhooked and he was barefoot. I prayed that the rubbing alcohol had worked.

"And what's the name of the school again, sir?" asked the boy in a voice so polite I thought I'd gag.

"Muckwater Middle School," said Papaw. "Same as this here mountain . . . Muckwater."

The boy nodded, and the poodle pranced and sniffed around the outhouse.

"Where'd you move from, boy?" asked Papaw as I stepped up beside him. Papaw ignored me, but the boy glanced at me and the dog snuffled my shoes.

"Spruce Knob, sir." The boy looked at me again, bug-eyed behind his thick lenses. "My father just got a foreman's job down at the glass factory in Swampville, and my mother is a dog breeder."

"Glass factory?" Papaw's ears pricked up at the word *glass*, while the part about the dog breeder got my attention.

"What kind of dogs?" I cut in, fiddling with my necklace. The boy's light-green eyes shifted like spun marbles, from Papaw to me to Papaw.

"Poodles," he said. "Toy poodles, just like this one." He reached down and patted the dog's curly fur, which put me in mind of the new perm Rose's mother got for Easter.

Papaw opened the outhouse door, exposing

his stack of *Stained Glassworkers* magazines piled up between the two toilets. "I work in glass, too," he said. "Stained glass." And then he stepped into the outhouse, pulling the door closed behind him.

I was mortified, standing there with that strange little dog and the even stranger boy. The boy and I watched the dog, which was mincing all around the outhouse and wiggling its stump of a tail.

"So," I said, "what's your name?"

"Dudley," said the boy in a stuffed-up kind of a voice. "Dudley Baxter." He yanked on the leash. "Sit, Suzette," he said to the dog.

Dudley? Suzette? I stifled a laugh, thinking that Dudley sure was a dud, all right, and that Suzette was no doubt the most persnickety pooch I ever saw.

"I want a dog," I said, "but not that kind of dog."

"Why not?" Dudley looked at me, his greasy black hair wet in the sunlight. Dudley put me in mind of a Milk Dud somebody chewed up a bit and then spit out.

"Well," I said, "I want a *real* dog, not a *toy* dog." Suzette was squatting in the weeds like a furry hop toad.

"Toy poodles are as real as the nose on my face," said the boy.

He had a point there, all right. Dudley had a nose like a beak. I reckon it had to be sturdy, to hold up those thick glasses.

"These dogs were used as waterfowl retrievers in France," said Dudley, in a tone that put waterfowl retrievers right up there next to God.

"Muckwater Mountain is a long way from France," I said.

Papaw came out of the outhouse. "What'd you say your name was again?" he asked, fastening the hooks on his overalls.

"Dudley Baxter, sir." The boy stuck out his hand as if he was offering a million bucks, obviously forgetting where Papaw had just been.

Papaw pumped his hand. "Glad to meet you, Dud," he said. "I'm Walter Bills, and this here is my granddaughter, Silver Nickles."

"Silver Nickles?" The Dud honked out a laugh that sounded more like a goose than a human being. "Could you loan me five cents, Silver Nickles?" he asked, his face all scrunched up like a rotten cauliflower.

"Very funny," I muttered. I'd already heard

every Silver Nickles joke in the book, along with those about my initials: SIN. Papaw was always harping on how hilarious it was for a religious person like me to have such a sinful monogram.

"Where do you live, Dud?" asked Papaw, scratching his armpit.

"Over on Stonecrest," said the Dud, tugging on Suzette's leash until I thought he'd strangle the mutt on that sequin-spangled collar of hers.

Papaw raised his eyebrows, which crawled above his eyes like two white woolly worms. "Stonecrest," he repeated. "Rich Folks' Rocks."

I stared at the Dud, trying to picture this sickly looking kid living in one of those glitzy houses perched up high in the rocks.

Papaw grinned. "Reckon your folks are rollin' in dough," he said, more a statement than a question. Leave it to Papaw to dig into other people's business as though it were his own personal truck patch.

The Dud frowned. "Money," he said, "isn't all it's cracked up to be."

Then, with those words from the Dud's blubbery lips, I was struck with an idea.

"Does your mother need any help with that dog breeding business of hers?" I asked. "I'm trying to earn money so that I can get my dream dog."

"Silver," growled Papaw.

The Dud shrugged. "You'll have to talk to my mother," he said. "She doesn't tell me much of anything."

I nodded. "Well," I said, "I'm heading inside. The *Sunday News* is waiting."

"Silver Nickles," Papaw called as I walked away, "you'll get a dog over my dead body."

I just turned and smiled, feeling the mustard-seed dome as sure as hope beneath my heart.

The Queen and the Castle

THE LADY EYED ME up and down from the doorway, taking in everything from the color of my hair to the holes eating their way through the toes of my sneakers. "Yes?" she asked in a voice so snobby you would have thought she was the queen of France or something. "May I help you?"

I took a big breath. "Yes, ma'am," I said, looking her deep in the eyes. Her eyes were small and hard and shiny, like sequins, with lots of purple eye shadow slathered on top. "My name is Silver Nickles, and I live over on Boghill Road. I'm in your son Dudley's class in school."

"Yes?" the lady replied, her eyes glazing over as if I bored her already. She ran a hand through her hair, which was black and tight and curly, like Suzette's.

"Well," I said, "Dudley told me that you own a dog breeding business."

"Stonecrest Kennels," the lady said, waving her hand at a purple-and-black sign hanging on the door behind her.

"Yes," I said, staring at the black poodle silhouetted on the sign. Something about this lady made me jittery, and I began to pick at my fingernails, a nervous habit I'd acquired when I lost my family.

Looking back at the lady, I jammed my hands into the pockets of my jeans. "I was wondering if you have any job openings," I said, the words tumbling from my mouth. "Like maybe helping to take care of the dogs?"

The lady lifted her chin into the air and batted her eyelids. "For yourself?" she asked.

I nodded. "I'm trying to earn money to buy a dog," I said, hoping to butter her up with this news. "I love dogs."

She fiddled with her earring, twisting the purple ball this way and that while gazing out somewhere over my head. I worried that maybe she could see Rose up on the hill, hiding out in the woods.

"I suppose," the lady said, shifting those hard eyes back in my direction again. Her eyes looked as if they were glued into the sockets. "I suppose you could clean the kennels. Minimum wage, Monday and Friday after school."

She didn't even ask what I thought of the deal, just laid down the law like a queen decreeing an order.

I nodded at the Queen, giving her my best fake smile.

"Thank you, ma'am," I said. "I'll be here on Monday."

"Wear old clothes," said the Queen. "Something like you're wearing now will do just fine."

I looked down, trying to see my jeans and shirt through the regal eyes of the Queen. *Old clothes?* These were some of my best school clothes.

"Thank you, ma'am," I said again and then lit off through the woods to find Rose.

"And what was *she* wearing?" asked Rose. That was just like Rose Roberts, more interested in the clothing than in the person underneath.

"Purple," I said. "All purple. She looked like a big old sour grape."

"*All* purple?" asked Rose, giggling.

"Yep." I nodded. "Purple eye shadow, purple

earrings, purple sweat suit in some kind of shiny stuff that rustled when she moved. Even her Stonecrest Kennels sign was purple."

Rose and I peered down through the trees. From where we hunkered on the hill, we could see the humongous house of stone where the Dud lived with his queen of a mother. The Castle. It was surrounded with a moat of rocks, those big, old Muckwater Mountain rocks that were about a million years old. Way down in the back, behind the Castle, we could see what must have been Stonecrest Kennels. The building had been painted pale purple with black doors and shutters. The place looked like a bruise—all purple and black—and it seemed to almost vibrate with the yip-yapping of poodles.

"I can't believe you're going to work there," said Rose, shaking her head.

I shrugged, snapping off a twig and swirling it through some mud. "Faith without works is dead," I said.

Rose rolled her eyes. "You and your stupid *faith*," she said.

"You and your stupid *magic*," I retorted, tossing the stick into the mud. "Magic won't bring me money. Faith won't bring me money. Neither your dreamcatcher earrings nor my mustard-seed necklace will bring me money. The only thing that'll bring me money, Rose, is *work*. And work is the only thing that'll bring me my dream dog."

Rose gazed down toward the Castle, sunshine glinting from her pink glasses. "And what about your papaw?" she asked. "He's probably the most bullheaded person in the world."

I cleared my throat and smiled. "The *second* most bullheaded person in the world," I said, pointing to myself. "I *will* get a dog, Rose Roberts, if it's the last thing I do on this earth."

The Little Prince

"**A**REN'T YOU THE MOST adorable eensy-weensy poo-poos?" cooed the Queen, bending over a litter of newborn puppies. "Oh, yes," she answered herself in that sickening-sweet baby talk. "Ooh is the most boootiful poo-poos."

Standing behind her, I rolled my eyes. The Queen talked a hundred times nicer to poodles than she did to people. She never even *looked* at the Dud, let alone *talked* to him.

"Bye-bye now, poo-poos," cooed the Queen, blowing kisses from her lilac-lipstick mouth. "I wuv ooo, poo-poos."

I groaned. *Poo-poos* was the right word for the Queen's poodles, that was for sure. Seemed all those poodles did was poop and pee and make messes in places they weren't supposed to.

I felt as though my job title at Stonecrest Kennels should have been pooper-scooper.

"How can you stand it?" Rose asked.

"A soul must do what a soul must do," I said, repeating one of Papaw's favorite sayings. "I reckon it's kind of like being a mother: you just take a deep breath and do what must be done. Do you think anybody really *likes* changing diapers?"

"Silver," Rose said, as though I was some kind of lunatic, "babies and dogs are two different things."

Well, you sure wouldn't know that by watching the Queen with her poo-poos. That lady loves those furry little critters a million times more than she loves her own son.

Poor Dud. I almost felt sorry for him, seeing how his mother ignored him and his father was never around. He must have felt so alone in that big, old, cold castle of a house, with the Queen dripping purple words and perfume all over the place.

"Bye-bye, poo-poos," said the Queen again, her shrill voice piercing my thoughts along with the doorbell. The Queen had this stupid system rigged up to the door of the kennels, where the doorbell said yip-yap instead of dingdong. I hated that doorbell, along with the way the Queen always kept Stonecrest Kennels all locked up.

"Come in," I called as the Queen went out and the Dud came in.

I watched while they passed in the doorway, not saying a word. I never in all my days saw a mother and son so unattached to each other.

"Hey, Silver Nickles," said the Dud with a big, goofy grin. The heavy, black door slammed shut behind him, automatically locked.

"Dud," I said, "I've been meaning to ask you something. Why does your mother lock this place up all the time?"

The Dud shrugged. "Why not?" he asked, running his fingers through his greasy black hair.

"Muckwater Mountain is safe," I said. "Papaw and I never lock our doors, even at night or when we leave the place empty. Nobody ever bothers around here."

"I don't know," the Dud said and shrugged again. "Maybe because of those snakes you see all over the mountain."

"Dud," I said, "those snakes aren't going to come strolling in the door like they're the Avon lady or something."

The Dud honked, his face all scrunched up.

That was the thing about the Dud: you could make the dumbest joke on earth, and he'd laugh as though you were the wittiest person on Muckwater Mountain. I reckon he was so glad to have somebody talking to him that he didn't even care about the conversation.

The Dud honked on and on. "The Avon lady," he kept saying, and then broke into a fresh fit of honking. When he finally finished, I lifted up one of the newborns.

"Meet the Little Prince," I said. I'd given him that name on account of the Queen raving on and on about his glossy black coat, as if he were her own offspring.

"Silver," the Dud hissed, squeaking across the floor. That was another thing about the Dud: he never lifted his feet when he walked, just slid them across those shiny purple and black tiles as if he were ice-skating in his sneakers. "You're not supposed to pick up a new puppy," said the Dud, screeching to a stop beside me and straightening his glasses.

"Why not?" I stroked the Little Prince's quivery body.

"Because," said the Dud, his dull, green eyes staring at me in horror, "if a human touches a new puppy, then the mother won't want it back."

I thought, *Is that what happened to you, Dud?* But what I said was, "Hogwash."

"Now," said the Dud, all indignant and self-righteous, *"you'll* have to be that puppy's mother."

"What?" I asked, almost dropping the little mutt. The Little Prince looked like a drowned mouse, if you asked me.

"You'll have to be that puppy's mother," the Dud said again.

I shoved the pup into the Dud's pale hands. "*You* be the mother," I said. "Or the father. Whatever. I told you before that I want a *real* dog, not a toy."

The Dud held the drowned mouse right up next to his sickly white face. "Toy poodles are as real as any other dog," he said. "They have a heart, a soul, and a tail." The Little Prince squeaked, proving my theory that he was really a mouse.

"I want a dog big enough to hug," I said. "A dog big enough so that I won't squish it if I roll over in my sleep some night. A dog big enough to protect me from *anything*."

The Dud rubbed the Little Prince across his nose. "Maybe you'll have a big dog someday, Silver," he said. "And being a mommy to this one will give you good practice."

I slid him a sideways look.

The Dud gently placed the pup among the other wiggling mice, all of them squirming over the mother as if she were a piece of cheese. "She'll still nurse him," said the Dud. "But after a couple of months, she won't want him."

A couple of months, I thought miserably. *Just in time for my birthday.*

"Dud," I said, "I don't want him, either."

The Dud's face cracked open with that big, goofy grin again. "In just a few months, Silver Nickles," he said, "you will be the proud mommy of a toy poodle."

"Over my dead body, Dud," I said. And then I yanked open that big, black door, heading toward home and away from the Dud and his yip-yapping toy poodles.

The Face at the Window

"I SWEAR, ROSE, there's something mighty strange about that place."

We were sprawled on Rose's bed, staring up at the white canopy floating like a cloud above our heads.

"The Dud lives there," said Rose. "He could make anywhere seem strange."

I shook my head. "It's not just that," I said. "The Queen keeps the kennels locked up tighter than a bank vault."

Rose shrugged. "Those toy poodles are probably worth a bundle," she said.

"And the father," I said, turning my head to look at Rose, "is never even there. Never."

"He's most likely at his job." Rose reached up and riffled her hand across the white fringes dangling from the canopy. Rose's birthstone ring glinted pink in the light from her reading lamp. For the life of me, I couldn't figure out why Rose had a reading lamp, with the little bit of reading she did. All Rose ever read was *Teen Fashions,* and that was more pictures than words anyway. But there was that lamp: all graceful and white and curved like the neck of a swan. The only light in *my* room came from a bare lightbulb glaring from the middle of my Dream Dog Display.

I leaned over and flicked off the reading lamp. "The Castle," I said, "gives me the creeps."

Rose stood and swayed over to her vanity table. "I got some new blush in the mail," she announced, as if imparting the news that she'd received a winner's check from the Publishers Clearing House sweepstakes. "Pink Passion. Want to try it?"

"No, thanks," I said, waving away the pink-frosted brush Rose brandished above me. I hated fake faces.

Rose shook her head. "You'd be so much prettier if you wore makeup," she said.

"But it wouldn't be *me* who was pretty," I said, hugging Rose's heart-shaped pillow. "It would be the *makeup*." I thought for a moment, stroking the pink satin pillow. "With Silver Nickles," I finally said, "what you see is the real thing. True as the sky is blue, no frills to fancy me up. As Papaw would say: the gen-u-ine article."

Rose was already sitting at her vanity, not even listening. *Vanity* hit the nail on the head, as far as Rose's makeup table was concerned. Vain as Miss America in the dressing room before the pageant, Rose had more makeup than she had skin to plaster it on. She had sticks for her lips and liners for her eyes and highlighters for goodness knows what. She had blush and mascara and foundation and powder, all leaving little rings and spills and smears on the pink wood tabletop. She had perfume and nail polish and hair gloss, enough to stock the shelves of the Kmart cosmetic aisle. And to think she was so stingy with her stuff that she had to snitch her mother's polish for Papaw's toenails. Why, Rose had enough nail polish to gussy up the entire United States Army, if she had a mind to.

"Rose," I said, watching her color her face like a paint-by-numbers picture, "don't you think beauty is only skin-deep?"

"Sure," said Rose, brushing black gunk across

her lashes until they spiked up like wet tar. She'd talked me into trying mascara one time, and my lashes ended up looking like fly legs.

"Well, I like to make my insides shiny," I said. "Even if the outside is as ugly as sin."

"Silver!" said Rose. Now she was working on the lips, drawing in a big, old, pouty, pink heart. As far as I was concerned, hearts belonged in the chest and not on the lips. Papaw always said that I wore my heart on my sleeve, but that was a bunch of baloney. I knew my heart stayed deep down inside of me, because I could feel it breaking. No sleeve heart would feel like that.

"My mama never wore makeup," I said softly, as Rose peered into that circle of light she used to magnify her face like a fun house mirror.

Rose turned to look at me. "She didn't?" she asked. "I thought *all* mamas wore makeup."

"Not mine," I said, hugging that heart-shaped satin pillow as if it could bring Mama back if I squeezed hard enough. "She wore pink nail polish, though, on her fingers and her toes. Always. When I was little, I used to think that her nails were naturally pink, on account of her shiny soul sparkling through. I always imagined that even Mama's *bones* were pink and glossy."

Rose just stared, and now that I had her attention, I kept on talking.

"Her eyes were brown like mine, like sunshine on swamp soil, she used to say. And her hair!" I closed my eyes. "Mama had the best hair. It was blond, I reckon, but not *just* blond. It was blond with kind of a clear light shining through, like fresh lemonade in a mason jar held to the sunshine. I used to think it was angel hair."

I opened my eyes and looked at Rose, who was real quiet, quieter than I'd ever known she could be.

"She was the best mama," I said, and the tears burned like fire behind my eyes.

"Why didn't you tell me about her before?" asked Rose. "We've been friends for a whole year."

I blinked, hard. "I reckon I wanted to keep her to myself for a while," I said. "I didn't want to share."

Just then, Rose's mother poked her face into the room, along with a pile of clean laundry. "Your clothes, Rose," she said, perfume wafting into the room along with her words. "Your father just called to tell you good night. He's working late."

"What else is new?" Rose sighed as Mrs. Roberts handed her the laundry and clicked off in her high heels.

I took a deep breath. "When Emmie was born," I said, "I didn't want to share my mama with her. I wanted Mama all to myself, just the way it always was for all those years. I loved Emmie—I really did—but I just didn't want to share. But you know what? I'd share my mama with a million babies, if only I could have her back."

Rose rubbed at her eyes, smearing her makeup, and I looked away. Staring at Rose's ruffly white curtains, so full of flounces and frills, I sighed. "I can't wait to see her again someday," I said. "In the sweet by-and-by."

Suddenly, something moved behind those ruffly white curtains. Something—or somebody—was standing outside in the dark, peering in through the window at Rose and me. A shadow, skimming past the glass and fading into the murky darkness of the yard.

I leaped up from the bed, quivering, and dashed to the window. Carefully parting the curtains, I peeked through the opening. It was raining, a fine May mist that glazed the windowpane and fogged the air.

"Silver," hissed Rose. "What on earth are you doing?"

"Somebody was out there," I whispered, "looking in the window."

Slowly opening the curtains, I stared into the night, as Rose crept up beside me. "It's gone," I said in a low voice, gazing at the drizzling haze outside. "Whatever it was."

Pastor Pete's Tattoo

IT WAS THE SUNDAY before Memorial Day, and Pastor Pete was talking about veterans, how we should respect and honor the soldiers who fought so hard for our country. Preaching about peace and war was one of Pastor Pete's favorite things, since he was a veteran himself—a Vietnam vet, as the tattoo on his arm said.

Pastor Pete went on and on about Biblical wars and such, as I stared at his tattoo. Red and white and blue, the tattoo flew from the bottom of his shirtsleeve: an American flag, with the word NAM blazing across the top. I always liked when the weather got warm enough for Pastor Pete to wear short-sleeved shirts to church, and I tried to bribe Rose into coming by bragging up Pastor Pete's tattoo. It didn't work.

"I never heard tell of a *preacher* with a *tattoo*," she said, as if a tattoo was something akin to a criminal record. "What kind of church is that anyway?"

"Full gospel," I said, knowing full well that full gospel was foreign talk to Rose Roberts.

"Well," she said, smug as all get-out, "Mama says it's a Holy Roller church, and one of these days the Muckwater Mountain Tabernacle of God is going to roll right off this mountain."

So I gave up. Neither hell nor high water nor Pastor Pete's tattoo could coax Rose into attending church every once in a blue moon. I gave up on Rose, but I still held some hope for Papaw. It seemed to me that after losing almost everybody he ever loved, church would be a comfort to Papaw.

"I need church like a hound dog needs a hankie," Papaw always said when I nagged him.

"Pastor Pete has a tattoo, Papaw," I told him once. "Just like you." Papaw had a blacksnake slithering up his arm, which always made me shudder. I hate snakes.

"Silver," said Papaw, running his fingers through his hair, "Pastor Pete and me have as much in common as a Chihuahua and a tired old hunting dog." Although it irritated me how

Papaw always used dogs to prove his point with me, I had to agree with that one. Jittery and high-strung, Pastor Pete was fidgety as they come, what with his knuckle-cracking and gum-snapping and hand-clapping. Seemed to me he was a whirlwind sent from Heaven, all swirled into the shape of a skinny little man with a Bible in his hand. I even wondered sometimes if his tattoo was really a brand sent straight from God. After all, spelled backward, it would be MAN.

Sitting in my usual spot in the back pew, I stared at Pastor Pete's flag until the colors blurred into a sort of purple smear, which made me think of the Queen, which made me think of the Dud, which made me think of the Little Prince, which made me think of my Dream Dog. Something about sitting in church made me prone to going off on a rampage of daydreaming, where one thought raced into another while I sat there looking as if I was listening. I blamed it on the back pew.

There was a kind of invisible line in the Muckwater Mountain Tabernacle of God. Nobody talked about that line, but nobody ever crossed it, either. It was the line dividing shack people like Papaw and me from house people like Rose, the Queen, and the Dud. Shack people included those who lived in trailers, old school buses, shanties, and tar paper shacks like ours. House people included middle-class families like the Robertses, who lived in a three-bedroom rancher, and high-class, highfalutin folks from over on Stonecrest.

It was funny about Muckwater Mountain, how you could walk a mile up Boghill Road and see everything from falling-apart shanties with rusty, old washing machines in the yard to nice, well-kept homes like Rose's to places like the Castle. Boghill Road kind of hardened into Stonecrest as it wound higher into the hills, where all the rich folks lived.

The Tabernacle of God was a mix of folks from all over the mountain, which is how a church should be. Only problem was that ridiculous invisible line, which Papaw said had been there even when Mama was little. The line was about three-quarters of the way toward the back of the church, straight across from the painting of Jesus. Poor people like me all sat in the back, behind that line. Rich folks sat up front, showing off their new clothes and hats and such. Most times, the back of the church wasn't all that crowded, and I figured the poor people had just given up on God. And that was sad.

I wasn't always in the back-of-the-church gang. Before Mama and Daddy died, we lived in a two-story frame house down in Swampville. It was a nice house—white with blue trim—snuggled right along the main street of town. Back then, I reckon I was middle-class, and I went to a church without a line. But that was all before, and this was now.

Right after the funeral, Papaw took me home to Muckwater Mountain. He couldn't afford the mortgage on our house in Swampville, on account of his stained-glass business being slow, and the house was sold.

Gazing at Pastor Pete, I began to tear at my fingernails. It always made me nervous: thinking of my old house, my old school, my old church. My old life.

Pastor Pete was still preaching on peace, and I wondered if he'd be marching in the Memorial Day parade down in Swampville. Papaw always did, showing off his ancient uniform that strained tight across the belly, decorated with buttons and medals and the Purple Heart Papaw was so proud of.

I smiled, thinking of the parade. It was so

short that you missed half of it if you blinked, but something about that parade always gave me chills. I loved the way the veterans marched along, looking straight and serious with their rifles and flags. The Swampville Elementary School band played "The Star-Spangled Banner," and the Scout troops carried flowers. Afterward, at the end of Main Street, there was the twenty-one-gun salute, with twenty-one soldiers firing into the air above the cemetery. Then it was over, with the Scouts scurrying around and putting flowers on the graves marked with tiny flags.

Still smiling, I doodled a flag in the corner of my church bulletin, thinking of how next year I'd have a dog for the Memorial Day parade. My dog and I would sit on the curb, right in front of my old house, and I wouldn't even miss my old life. We'd eat hot dogs from the fire hall and wait for the drums to start. I'd loop the leash like a bracelet around my wrist, feeling safe and happy and loved. I'd rub my dog's ears and comfort him when the gunshots boomed across the graveyard, not even flinching at the sound.

I was thinking all this, and smiling and doodling away, when something cut into my daydream. It was the Dud, sliding into the pew next to me and grinning his big, goofy grin. He was all decked out in a bow tie, jacket, and baggy black pants, with his hair slicked back like a Vitalis commercial. His face had a new crop of zits, and he smelled like cologne. My smile fell to the floor and I sighed, wishing this was just my imagination. But no, it was the Dud . . . in the flesh and grinning and smelling as though he'd tried every sample spray bottle in Kmart.

"Hey, Silver Nickles," he whispered, scooting closer until his bony elbow was jabbing my side. "Mommy of the Little Prince," he added, his blubbery lips almost touching my ear.

I swatted at my ear as if chasing off a pesky fly, rolling my eyes and glaring at the Dud.

And then it hit me: The Dud had crossed the line.

10

The Dud's First Parade

IT WAS LATE AFTERNOON on Memorial Day, and we were packed like sardines in the cab of Papaw's pickup truck: Papaw, Rose, the Dud, and me.

"A Rose between two thorns," Papaw said, nudging Rose in the ribs and snickering. Memorial Day always put Papaw in a good mood.

"Mountaineers are always free," hollered Papaw, grinding gears as we headed down Boghill Road toward Swampville. That saying about mountaineers was West Virginia's state motto and one of Papaw's favorites. He always said it when he was feeling footloose and fancy-free, like today. I couldn't see how he felt so free, all buttoned up in that tight old uniform.

Papaw belched and the Dud honked. Leave it to the Dud to laugh at something sick like that. I rolled my eyes and hung my head out the window, smelling sugar maple and exhaust fumes. Papaw's old truck was about as gassy as Papaw. I prayed that he'd have enough horse sense not to pass gas in crowded conditions like these.

"Your grandpa is so funny," wheezed the Dud, honking away.

I ignored him, hoping that he'd get lost in the crowd once we got to Swampville.

Papaw stuck a wad of chew in his mouth, a disgusting habit that irritated me to no end. "You're going to end up with cancer of the mouth," I muttered. "Just like Uncle Jake."

Papaw shrugged, his Purple Heart swinging. "Got to die of something," he said.

I shuddered, hating how he tossed around the idea of his dying as if discussing a day trip to White Sulphur Springs. "I hate when you say that, Papaw," I said, craning my neck to look around Rose and the Dud.

Papaw shifted his chew to the other cheek. "A soul's got to do what a soul's got to do," he said.

I sighed and looked out the window, leaning against the door as Papaw made a right turn into Swampville. I didn't want the Dud and me careening bodies like bumper cars, and I kept pressing my legs toward the door. I was actually getting tired, working so hard not to touch the Dud.

"I wish my parents came to the parade," pouted Rose with her pink lips, as we swung onto Main Street. I rolled my eyes, knowing full well that the only reason Rose Roberts came to Swampville was to look for boys. She said there was a better selection in town.

Papaw found a parking spot at the fire hall, and the Dud actually clapped his hands, applauding as if Papaw had just performed a miracle before our very eyes.

"My first parade," he guffawed, jabbing at his glasses.

Rose and I gawked at him from both sides. "*What*?" I asked. "You've never been to a parade in your *entire life?*"

"I've never been to a parade," he said, smoothing down his slimy hair. "My parents never have time."

Papaw's old Ford grumbled to a stop, coughing almost as bad as Papaw. "Just think,"

I said as we all piled from the truck, "by this time next year, I'll have my dog."

"Silver," growled Papaw, "you'll have a dog over my dead body."

I rattled my mustard seed, winking at Rose as we walked down Main Street with the Dud trailing behind. Papaw stayed at the fire hall, where all the old soldiers ganged up before the parade.

"The Little Prince," hissed the Dud. That boy was like gum on my shoe; I just couldn't shake him.

"Want to see my old house?" I asked Rose, paying no mind to the Dud, who was chanting "Mommy of the Little Prince" from somewhere behind us.

Rose stopped dead in her tracks. "Your old house?" she asked. "Silver, we've been through this town a million times, and you never told me this was where you used to live."

I stopped and looked at her. "There's a time for everything," I said, "and today is the time." The Dud kept on walking and gawking, and next thing I knew he banged right into me in a rear-end collision.

I turned and glared at him. "What's your problem, Dud?" I asked. "Don't those Coke bottle bottoms work?" I reached back and tapped one of his lenses.

The Dud took off his glasses and looked at me. "They work," he said. "Because now I can't even see how pretty you are."

Rose hooted and I blushed, watching the Dud clean his lenses on the tail of his shirt. Without his goofy glasses, the Dud wasn't half bad-looking. His eyes were kind of a jelly-bean green, bigger and brighter in the light. And his nose wasn't quite so beaklike, without those heavy black glasses to squash it down and out. Even his hair looked better somehow, without those shiny black rims magnifying the greasiness. Only problem was, those pimples still splattered across his pale face like dots of elderberry jelly.

Rose elbowed me, snickering, and the Dud put his glasses back on. Now he was back to being the Dud, the plain old goofy, bug-eyed Dud.

"My house is over this way," I said, taking Rose's arm and turning away from the Dud. We walked down Main Street, the Dud wheezing along behind us. I swear, that boy must have had the worst case of allergies on Muckwater Mountain. Sometimes I wondered if he was maybe allergic to *himself*.

"Dud," I said as we headed toward my old house, "would it be possible to pick up your feet when you walk? You work on my nerves."

The Dud didn't answer, just shuffled along the sidewalk like a ninety-year-old man, huffing and puffing.

"Well," said Rose, "where is it?"

I stopped. "There," I said, staring. It was still there, as tall and white as ever, the blue shutters bright like springtime sky. It looked like a mansion.

There was a family on the porch: a mama, a daddy, two girls, and a dog. They were sitting on the steps, waiting for the parade, I reckon. The mama and daddy were holding hands, and the bigger girl was reading a book, *Maniac Magee* by Jerry Spinelli. I was so close I could read the cover.

"When does the parade start?" asked the smaller girl, who was brushing the dog and dropping balls of matted fur into the yard.

"Soon, honey," said the mama as we walked by. "Soon."

I blinked hard and swallowed the tears. I hadn't been that close to my old house since I lived there. I could still see my bedroom: blue and white just like the house, with a built-in bookshelf and a walk-in closet. I could see the nursery, all done up in rocking horses and soft, pink stuff. I could see me in that house, and Emmie, and Mama and Daddy.

Rose and the Dud were behind me now, whispering. I turned and looked at them, rubbing my eyes.

"Where should we sit for the parade?" I asked. People were passing by us now, finding spots on the curb and plopping down on blankets and lawn chairs.

"Silver," said Rose, touching my arm. "Why don't you ask those people if you can go inside the house? You know, look around and see your old bedroom . . ." She trailed off.

"I can see it in my mind," I said, pulling away and pushing forward. Rose and the Dud followed, and I could *feel* them giving each other looks behind my back. *Poor pitiful Silver*, I could hear them thinking. *The girl without a family. The girl who's stuck on Muckwater Mountain in a two-room tar paper shack. The girl without a dog.* I sighed, wondering why on earth they'd even want a friend like me, such a pathetic and pitiful soul. I stopped.

"Listen," I said, turning around and surprising them. "It's not my house anymore. It wouldn't be the same. I hardly ever think about it, and I don't want to start now. Understand?"

They nodded, like two puppets on the same string, even though I knew that neither one had the foggiest idea what I was talking about. Drums thumped from somewhere down the street, and I found a spot on the curb.

"Is this okay?" I asked, and they both nodded again. I smiled, knowing that I had Rose Roberts and Dudley Baxter wrapped around my little finger.

We sat down on the concrete, watching Main Street for the first sight of the parade. The Dud grinned and clapped his hands and stomped his feet in rhythm to the drumbeat. "My first parade," he said. "I thought you said they have hot dogs," he whined, looking at me.

"Dud," I said, "if you went for a hot dog now, you'd miss the parade."

"Don't want to do that," said the Dud, picking at a zit. I scooted farther away from him and stared down Main Street.

"Here it comes," I said. "The parade." I loved this parade, which had been going on for as far back as I could remember. Why, I could recall being three years old and sitting on Daddy's shoulders to see the soldiers.

"Here comes the band," hollered the Dud over "The Star-Spangled Banner." People looked at him, then back at the street, and I moved as far away from the Dud as I could without looking as though I was in love with Rose.

"And there are the Boy Scouts," I said, pointing.

"And the veterans!" yelled the Dud, standing up and saluting. I put my head between my knees, hoping that nobody from my old school saw me with this hollering moron of a Milk Dud.

"Hey," said Rose, rubbernecking after the Boy Scouts. "Did you see that guy with the blond hair, there in the back row?"

"Rose," I said, "we're here to watch the parade." Papaw was marching by, staring straight ahead with his rifle held smartly on his shoulder. I looked at Papaw, with all his medals and his Purple Heart and his lined old face, and suddenly I felt like crying. Just crying and crying until next Memorial Day, or maybe the one after.

"Hey, Mr. Bills," shouted the Dud, still saluting like an idiot. Papaw ignored him and just kept on marching toward the cemetery with the rest of his old military buddies.

"Shut up, Dud," I said, as we stood and followed after the parade. "If you do that in the cemetery, you're dead."

The Dud honked. "If I do that in the cemetery, I'm dead," he kept saying as we walked. "You're so funny, Silver Nickles." Honk, honk. I was afraid I'd kill him if I heard that confounded honk one more time today.

We finally got to the cemetery, where everybody stood silent and still, waiting for the twenty-one gun salute. Even the grave markers seemed to be expecting something, all lined up in rows of stone. I tried not to look toward the back, along the fence, where Mama's and Daddy's and Emmie's bodies were buried side by side. I concentrated on staring at the flags flapping crisply in the breeze.

Suddenly, the first gunshot exploded, and I jumped like always. Then, another . . . and another . . . with a bugle moaning Taps sad and slow as the shots rang out one by one.

I looked around, seeing the Scouts hugging bouquets of flowers and the soldiers standing at attention and the band members with their hands over their hearts. Familiar sights on Memorial Day, these things were imprinted in my memory along with the sound of the shots.

But then, as I gazed around, I saw something strange. Papaw was clutching his chest and dropping down to the ground, as lifeless and limp as a fallen soldier in the Swampville cemetery.

11

Everybody's Going to Die Someday

You'll get a dog, Silver, over my dead body. The words echoed through my mind again and again, like the gunshots, as we all stood looking down at Papaw in his hospital bed.

"You know what I thought for a minute?" guffawed the Dud, crossing his scrawny arms. "I thought that he was shot. That those were *real* guns." Honk, honk.

"Dud," I said, "this is no time for honking. I mean, laughing." Papaw was hooked up to about a zillion bottles and monitors and tubes.

"Maybe it was that sliver of shrapnel in his knee," Rose said. "Maybe it moved up to his heart and gave him a heart attack."

"Rose," I said, "this is no time for joking."

"Who's joking?" asked Rose, primping in the mirror above Papaw's bed.

I sighed. Those two were like clowns in a circus act, joshing around when *normal* people would be crying. "Why don't you two go take a walk?" I asked, sitting down slowly on Papaw's bed.

"Well," said the Dud, fishing around in the pocket of his baggy shorts, "I was thinking of taking a stroll to the vending machines out in the lobby." Maybe he finally got the hint.

Rose heaved her big pink purse onto her shoulder. "See you in a little while, Silver. If you need anything, just holler."

If I need anything. I need Papaw to open his eyes and to be okay. I need him not to die, not to leave me alone in Bark Shanty.

I sighed, thinking of how important a dog had been only a few hours ago. Now my dream dog didn't mean a hill of beans. I'd gladly give every penny I earned working at Stonecrest Kennels, just to make Papaw be okay. *Please let him be okay, Lord. Please let him be okay.* The prayer ran through my body like blood, on and on and on.

I leaned over the bed and smoothed down Papaw's fuzzy white hair. "Come on, Papaw," I said, as a nurse bustled around checking his connections, "open your eyes. I promise I'll never paint your toenails again." The nurse didn't even blink; I reckon she'd heard all kinds of outlandish things, there in Swampville Hospital.

"I'll never get irritated with you again, Papaw," I said. "You can belch and pass gas and snore and chew and chase me with your choppers all you want." Papaw got a big kick out of pretending his dentures were going to bite me, clicking them together like the castanets we clapped in music class.

"Wake up, Papaw," I pleaded. "If you wake up and come home, I'll buy you a whole slew of peanut-butter eggs. I'll help with your stained glass and mow the front yard. I'll weed the garden and clean the kitchen and chop wood. Shoot, I'll even rip down my entire Dream Dog Display." I paused, waiting for Papaw to jump up and down and spit wooden nickels, as he always said he would if I'd stop pestering him for a hound dog.

"Pa-paw," I said in a soft sing-song kind of voice, gentle like a lullaby. "Oh, Papaw. Wake up, Papaw. I'll stop nagging you about church, I swear. Cross my heart and hope to die." I cringed, wishing I hadn't said that word.

"Don't stop nagging about church, Silver," said a deep voice from behind, scaring the daylights out of me. "Pester him until kingdom come, if that's what it takes."

It was Pastor Pete, sneaking up behind me. He was wearing an orange shirt and blue shorts, with blue-striped socks, and looked different in the hospital from the way he did in church. Smaller and skinnier somehow.

"Pastor Pete," I said, sitting up straighter. "What are you doing here?"

"This is my job, Silver," he said, making a beeline for Papaw and touching his hand. "I was at the parade and knew that the ambulance took someone to the hospital. Soon as I found out it was Brother Walt, I hightailed it over here in two shakes of a lamb's tail." He cracked his knuckles and then pulled a tiny Bible from his shirt pocket.

I stared at his tattoo. "Is Papaw going to die?" I asked, my voice sounding too loud in the air-conditioned room of white.

"Everybody's going to die someday, Silver," said Pastor Pete matter-of-factly, as if he was informing me that everybody goes to Kmart. "Death is a fact of life; we just never know when it's going to happen. The Lord doesn't hand out schedules." He smiled and unwrapped a piece of gum, popping it into his mouth.

"Bubblicious?" he asked, holding out a chunk.

"No, thanks," I replied, wondering how anybody could think of blowing bubbles at a time like this.

"I talked to the doctors on my way in," mumbled Pastor Pete, the words getting stuck in the wad of watermelon gum. "They say it was a mild heart attack. He should be home within the week."

"The *week?*" I asked, thinking *What about me?*

Pastor Pete nodded, blowing a huge, pink bubble. It popped. "Do you know anybody you could stay with for the week?"

At that moment, Rose and the Dud made their grand entrance, slurping on sodas: diet Coke for Rose and Minute Maid Grape for the Dud. It was funny how I noticed crazy little details at a time like that, with Papaw in the hospital and all.

"Hey, Silver Nickles," said the Dud, a ring of purple above his upper lip. "Hey, Pastor Pete."

Rose stopped dead, staring at Pastor Pete. Her eyes moved from his face to his tattoo to his shorts to his sneakers. "He doesn't *look* like a preacher," she said.

The Dud honked. "What is a preacher supposed to look like?" he asked, sloshing some of his soda from the can as he tried to shake Pastor Pete's hand.

"Mr. Bills still out cold?" asked the Dud, gawking down at Papaw.

Pastor Pete nodded. "He's on some pretty strong medication," he said, blowing another bubble.

"I reckon I could stay with Rose," I blurted out. "If it's okay with her parents."

Rose looked at me. "What?" she asked.

"I need a place to stay for about a week," I said. "Until Papaw comes home." *If he comes home. Please, Lord, let Papaw be okay. I'll promise anything, if only Papaw gets better.*

Rose waved her hand. "It'll be fine," she said. "My parents like Silver Nickles."

"Do they like copper pennies, too?" asked the Dud, grinning his big, stupid grin.

"Dud," I said, my teeth tight, "this is no time for your dumb jokes."

Pastor Pete smiled. "I'll drive you kids home," he said, putting his hand on Papaw and opening his Bible.

I held my mustard-seed dome to my mouth, breathing on it as if breathing life back into Papaw.

"Pastor Pete," I said, "do you know that Bible verse about faith like a grain of mustard seed?"

Pastor Pete cracked his gum and snapped open his Bible. "Matthew 17:20," he said. "If ye have faith as a grain of mustard seed, ye shall say unto this mountain, Remove hence to yonder place; and it shall remove; and nothing shall be impossible unto you."

The Dud jabbed at his glasses. "Wow," he said. "Faith could move Muckwater Mountain. Imagine that."

Rose just rolled her eyes, as Pastor Pete closed his and said a prayer over Papaw. "A-men," he said in closing.

"A-*man*," I whispered. A dog no longer mattered; everything that meant anything in this world to me was lying there still and silent in the form of about 180 pounds of man. Papaw. My Papaw. *You'll be okay, Papaw, I know you will. I have faith. I have faith a zillion times bigger than this puny little grain of mustard seed. I have faith like a whole mountain of watermelon seeds, Papaw. I have faith and you'll be okay—I know you will. I hope.*

12

Now I Lay Me Down to Sleep

IT WAS ALMOST MIDNIGHT on the night before the last day of school, and I couldn't sleep.

I'd had trouble sleeping all week: Monday, Tuesday, Wednesday, Thursday, Friday, Saturday. And now Sunday . . . the day I'd set my sights upon for Papaw to be home. Sunday just wasn't Sunday without Papaw, and tomorrow it would be a week since Papaw's heart attack. Weak heart or no weak heart, I wanted him home. And I wanted him home *now*. After all, Pastor Pete had said a *week*, and Pastor Pete's word was gospel, in my book. The heck with all those doctors and their fancy heart-monitoring equipment. Papaw's heart belonged in Bark Shanty with me, not down in Swampville Hospital at the mercy of anybody in a white uniform who wanted to take a poke at it.

I missed Papaw. I missed Papaw, and I missed my bed, and I missed my Dream Dog Display. I missed my stained-glass window and the old wardrobe squatting in the corner. I missed home.

Tomorrow was the last day of school, the only day of the year we were allowed to have water fights on the bus. Percy the bus driver had promised to stop at Mud Creek on the way home so that we could all fill our water jugs. Then we could throw the water all over one another and all over the old school bus. Percy said it gave the bus a good washing.

11:57. Rose's clock radio glowed the numbers into the night like a warning: Time to Go to Sleep. 11:58. I buried my face in the cool silkiness of the pillow.

"Now I lay me down to sleep," I said out loud. "I pray the Lord my soul to keep. Thy love go with me through the night, and wake me with the morning light. Amen."

"Len?" Rose muttered beside me, sighing and flopping over. I hated sleeping with Rose, on account of her sleep-talking and such. All I'd heard all week was "Len, Len, Len." Rose was head over heels for this boy in school, Len Ryler, who sat right behind her in homeroom.

"No, I didn't say Len," I snapped, scooting over to the edge of the bed. "I said Amen."

"Len?" asked Rose again, rolling over and snuggling up next to me. I shoved her back to her side, heaving her around and around like a sack of flour.

Squeezing shut my eyes, I wondered how it would be to get married and *have* to sleep in the same bed with someone else for the rest of my life. Considering how Rose yakked in her sleep and drooled all over the pillows and swam like a fish across the bed, I decided to never get married. It wasn't worth the loss of sleep.

I'd felt like a zombie all week, tired and dull and slow. I'd failed my English test, which wasn't me at all but the zombie in my body. My *body* didn't even seem like me, because I'd been wearing Rose's clothes all week. She tried to con me into makeup, too, but I downright refused. There was no way in this world that Silver Nickles was putting on a false face.

"I bet that a little blush and a bit of lipstick would fetch you a boyfriend just like that," Rose said, snapping her fingers.

"Rose," I said, "I don't want a boyfriend."

"I want a doggie," Rose said, mocking me in a shrill little baby voice. "I want a doggie to love. I want to smooch a pooch."

That's what I need, I thought, floundering around in Rose's bed at 12:02 on Sunday night. *I need Woof-Woof.* I need something to hug, something from home, something familiar.

12:03. I decided that tomorrow, after school, I'd stop by Bark Shanty and pick up my toy dog.

It was 12:04. The shining red numbers only made me feel more awake, so I turned the clock around backward. *There, I fixed you,* I thought, rolling onto my stomach. Ouch, my mustard-seed dome was hard against my chest. I flipped it onto my back and closed my eyes.

"I can't believe you're wearing that stupid necklace to bed," Rose said the first night.

"Well, I can't believe you're wearing face paint to bed," I retorted, buttoning up the white cotton nightgown Rose loaned me. At home, I wore old T-shirts to bed.

"And a *bra*," Rose said, brushing her hair the 100 times she insisted made it shine. "*Nobody* wears a bra to bed."

"Silver Nickles does," I said. Actually, this was the first time, but Rose didn't need to know that.

I changed positions, rolling onto my back and moving the mustard seed again. Opening my eyes, I thought the sky was falling, just for a split second. That had happened every night, when I opened my eyes and saw all that cloudy white stuff hanging over my head.

Staring at the canopy, I pretended that my Dream Dog Display was up there. "Rufus and Rex and Romeo," I recited in a whisper. "Sargent and Sancho and Snowy. Herbert Hoover and Harry Houdini and Hemingway."

"Len's away?" muttered Rose, snorting through her nose.

"Yes, Rose," I said, heaving myself up from the bed. "Len's away. He's gone forever, flew away to live on the moon."

"In my room?" mumbled Rose.

"Uh-huh," I said, walking to the window. It was a full moon tonight, or something mighty close. I pulled back the curtains and looked into the sky, thinking how folks always said crazy things happened during a full moon—stuff like werewolves and vampires and ghosts, stuff I didn't believe in but that somehow seemed more real this late at night, in somebody else's house.

I shivered and slammed down the storm window, even though the air was warm. It smelled like June: all lilacs and mountain laurel and lawn mower fumes. Crickets were chirping to beat the band, which cheered me up somewhat. I love crickets.

I stood there at the window, just staring up at the smirking circle of moon, the same moon that swung in the sky over at Swampville Hospital and over Bark Shanty. "Goodnight, Papaw," I said out loud and pulled the curtains shut.

But as I did, something caught my eye from out in the yard. It was a man, leaping from tree to tree, hiding behind the trunks so as not to be seen. I held my breath, shaking.

"Rose," I hissed, as the man dashed from the yard and into the woods. "Wake up."

But it was already too late. The man was gone, vanished into the June air, as if nothing had ever been there.

13

A Hug from the Dud

"YOU'VE BEEN READING too many ghost stories, Silver." Rose flicked open her mirror compact and fussed with her blush.

"Rose, I swear on my life that somebody was out there," I said. "A man."

Rose's dreamcatchers swayed back and forth with the motion of the school bus. Old Number 36 was one of the most rickety buses, on account of climbing the worst parts of Muckwater Mountain day in and day out.

Propping my knees on the green seat before me, I continued. "I know it for a fact, Rose. The moon was full, and the yard was lit up like a football stadium. I saw the guy with my very own eyes, hopping from tree to tree."

"Are you sure it wasn't a jackrabbit?" Rose

asked, still gawking into that little pink compact of hers. I couldn't for the life of me understand why she was so worried about her makeup when it was only going to wash off in the water battle.

"No, Rose," I said. "It wasn't a jackrabbit." My stomach churned, all full of pizza and potato chips and pickles and punch.

"Well, how do you know it was a *man?*" Rose asked, finally snapping closed her compact and looking at me. "How do you know it wasn't just a kid?"

"What would a kid be doing out there at midnight?" I asked.

Rose shrugged. "What would a man be doing out there at midnight?" she asked. "I still say it's just too many ghost stories."

"I give up," I said, yawning and slumping down in the seat. "Maybe next time you'll see for yourself." I closed my eyes, trying to block out all the hooting and hollering sounds of the last day of school.

The bus rattled and rumbled, grinded gears and grumbled, and pretty soon the motion and the sounds became a comfort to me, like some kind of loud lullaby. I took long, slow breaths and tried to imagine that I was a baby, being rocked to sleep in the seat of Number 36. The breeze from the half-open windows was gentle and calming on my face, and sunshine warmed my legs like a quilt. Passing trees made patterns that darkened my eyelids for a minute and then danced past. I sighed and drifted into sleep.

I was dreaming about swimming. It was a big pool, with lots of screaming kids and a slide and a diving board. I was diving, a beautiful and graceful jackknife that made everybody ooh and aah. "She should be in the Olympics," somebody said, and next thing I knew, I was awake and drenched. Soaking wet and freezing cold, sitting there gasping and wiping my eyes. I was shell-shocked and dizzy, not knowing where the water came from. And then I saw: the Dud. He was standing in the aisle of the school bus with a cutoff milk jug in his hand and creek water dripping from his greasy hair.

"Surprise, Silver Nickles," he snickered, turning the jug upside down over my head. A few drops trickled out and landed on my nose, as the Dud hightailed it up the aisle and out the door.

I sputtered and muttered for a minute, and then I shot into action. I grabbed my jug, stood up dripping, and headed for the exit. The bus was empty; all the kids were in the creek. I stumbled down the slippery steps and looked around for the Dud. He was there: hiding by the side of Mud Creek behind a tree, as if that skinny little tree trunk could hide his white-paste face.

I lit off for the Dud, hooking him from the side of his scrawny little body and dragging him toward the creek. I swear, that boy was as weak as a twice-used teabag. He felt like a fence post in my hands, all stiff and straight with his toothpick arms locked into place beside him.

"Revenge is a bugger, isn't it, Dud?" I asked, yanking him down into the mucky creek where everybody said the snakes were as long as a tall man's arm. I shuddered, trying to hold the Dud in the water without getting in too deep myself.

The Dud was shivering, and I could see goose bumps popping up all over his pale twig arms. "Cold, Dud?" I asked, pushing on his bony shoulders from behind.

And then the Dud did something that surprised me. Surprised me and confounded me and made me madder than a wet hen, all in one fast move. Whipping around and shaking loose his shoulders, the Dud grabbed me and held me in a hug, right smack-dab up against his skin-and-bones chest. Stupefied, I just stood there for a split second, feeling the pounding of his heart and the tightening of his arms pressing against my back. The Dud was hugging me, clinching me in his arms like a spider capturing a fly. But this was one fly who was going to fight for her life. I jerked away and flailed at the Dud, punching him and smacking him and jabbing him in his caved-in little stomach. I really let him have it, socking and slapping away. "Now you pay, Dud," I said, clenching my teeth. "Now you pay."

"No," said the Dud, taking off his glasses. "Now *you* pay."

I stopped. The Dud's goofy black glasses were broken, snapped in half like a bent pencil.

"Now you pay, Silver Nickles," said the Dud, sticking the glasses in his pocket. "I hope you have lots of silver nickels, Silver Nickles." He honked, his green eyes all squinty beneath his wet hair.

I took a deep breath, still feeling those spider arms closing me in. "It's your own fault, Dud," I said, as Percy waved everybody back on the bus.

I stomped up the steps and down the aisle, rolling my eyes at Rose. "The Dud hugged me," I hissed, sliding into the seat beside her.

"He *what?*" Rose yipped, her eyes wide circles of blue.

"Sshhh," I said, looking around the bus. "The Dud grabbed me and gave me a hug," I said under my breath, picking at my fingernails. "It was disgusting."

Rose squealed. "I knew you'd have a boyfriend before you had a dog," she whispered, giggling.

"The Dud is not my boyfriend," I said, gritting my teeth and wiping water from my face. "I don't want a boyfriend. I don't *need* a boyfriend." I wrung out my hair. "I need a boyfriend like a hound dog needs a hankie," I said, smug.

Number 36 started with a roar and rumbled up the mountain, practically shaking with kids screaming and hollering and cheering. "No more lessons, no more books, no more teachers' dirty looks!" yelled the Dud, making more of a fool of himself.

"Your boyfriend is a moron," Rose said, pulling the compact from her humongous pink purse.

I ignored her, leaning forward. The bus was inching up Boghill Road toward Bark Shanty. "Percy," I called. "I'm getting off at home today."

Rose looked at me, stunned. I smiled, realizing that I hadn't told Rose about fetching Woof-Woof. She thought I was mad at her for bedeviling me about the Dud. Well, she could just think that for a while. Served that razzing Rose Roberts right, to think I was so provoked that I'd spend the night alone in Bark Shanty.

Number 36 squeaked to a stop, the door swinging open. "See you in September, Percy," I said, ignoring Rose.

"See you tonight at the kennels," squawked the Dud from his front-row seat. "Better work hard and earn lots of silver nickels, Silver Nickles, because *now you pay.*" Honk, honk.

I looked up at the Dud, whose naked eyes gleamed bright and green up at me. Shaking my head, I started down the steps but looked back. The Dud winked and then blew a kiss from his blubbery lips.

"Disgusting," I muttered and stepped off the bus. The door closed, and the bus roared off up the mountain, taking Rose and the Dud with it. "Good riddance," I mumbled, wading across the yard. The grass had really grown during the week Papaw was in the hospital.

Pulling open the front door, I took a deep breath. *Home*, I thought, *home, sweet home.*

During the past eight days, I'd finally come to realize how much Bark Shanty was home. Bark Shanty and Papaw.

And now, without Papaw, Bark Shanty seemed empty and hollow inside, like one of those hollow chocolate Easter bunnies. The shell was still there, but the sweetness inside was gone. It was quiet, only the ticking of Mamaw's old cat clock and the hum of the icebox to break the silence.

"Home, sweet home," I said out loud, hoping to talk some life back into the place. It didn't work; Bark Shanty didn't answer.

I wandered into my room, where the air smelled stale and old. It's a strange feeling to go back to a place where you were just before something life-changing happened, to go there again after it happened. Eerie somehow, like going back in time.

I looked around at the bed and the wardrobe and the desk, crouched beneath the stained-glass window. There was my Dream Dog Display, looking like something from another lifetime. I flopped on my bed, thinking how I'd gladly trade my Dream Dog Display for Papaw's health, any day. I hadn't even bothered looking for the adoption column in yesterday's newspaper, as Rose's parents had taken me to visit Papaw in the afternoon. He looked good, all bright-eyed and bushy-tailed and ready to get the heck out of there.

I picked up Woof-Woof and hugged him, and then slowly wound the key on his belly. "How much is that doggie in the window," I sang softly, holding Woof-Woof tight and close until the music tinkled to a stop.

"How much *is* that doggie in the window?" I said, walking to the wardrobe. I'd count my money and see just how much I had saved. Pulling open the door, I reached up and grabbed my money can from the shelf. Every Monday and Friday, the Queen paid me in cash, which I brought right on home and stashed in the Maxwell House coffee can.

Flipping off the plastic lid, I reached deep in the can, thinking that I most likely had enough for the stuff I really needed. The rawhide chews and puppy food and the sturdy red leash. The blue bowl and the collar with a bell. The shampoo and the powder and the brush and the ball and the bone. Forget about the fancy doghouse and the soft, plushy doggie bed. The dog would probably sleep in my bed anyway. I smiled, thinking of Papaw coming home from the hospital and being greeted by all that hound dog loot—the fruits of my labor—piled high on the kitchen table.

But my smile faded as I fished around in the coffee can and found nothing. All my money was gone.

14

Bark Shanty, By Heart

THE COFFEE CAN CLATTERED to the floor, and I sank onto the bed, shaking. Who could have taken my money? Nobody ever got robbed on Muckwater Mountain. Nobody, that is, but Silver Iris Nickles.

I put my head in my hands and tried to think of everybody and anybody who knew that Papaw was in the hospital. Rose, the Dud, Rose's parents, the Dud's parents, Percy, Pastor Pete, all the kids on the school bus, the entire congregation of the Muckwater Mountain Tabernacle of God. It could have been anybody, although I really didn't consider Pastor Pete to be a suspect.

Pastor Pete. I'd call Pastor Pete. Maybe if he prayed fast enough, the thief would be caught and I'd get my money back. *Wishes and prayers, they don't change things a bit.* I could still hear Papaw's voice on Easter morning, and see his eyes. Well, I'd open Papaw's eyes and show him just how much prayer *could* change things.

Faith, I thought. *Have faith. Everything will be okay. Papaw will come home, the money will come back, I'll have my dog. Faith. If you have faith as a grain of mustard seed, nothing shall be impossible unto you. Faith . . . faith.*

Clasping my hands, I reached for my mustard seed. It was gone, *my mustard-seed necklace was gone.*

I gasped, and tears burned my eyes. My money was gone, my papaw was gone, and now my necklace was gone. It seemed that everything that meant anything was being yanked from my life by some unseen thief.

Sobbing, I stood shakily and staggered to the kitchen. Halting by our old, black, wall telephone, I leaned against the logs, reeling, and tried to remember Pastor Pete's telephone number. And then I remembered that Pastor Pete lived right across the road, in the basement of the church.

Stumbling through the door, I wallowed through the muddy yard and across Boghill

Road, to the church. Dashing around back, I pounded on the apartment door.

"Pastor Pete!" I yelled. "I've been robbed."

Nothing. No answer. I rattled the doorknob. It was locked. "Pastor Pete!" I called again, peeking in through the window. It was silent and still.

I sighed, turned around and headed home. Rose. I'd call Rose. She'd know what to do.

Sweating and out of breath, I flung open our flimsy front door, thinking of how easily the thief had done the same thing. Breathing fast and furious, I thought that the air inside Bark Shanty smelled different somehow now than it had when I'd come home ten minutes ago. It smelled *invaded*, full of somebody who had no right to be there. It even *felt* strange in the place, as if somebody spooky was slinking about and hiding in the corners. I looked around, scanning the floor for my mustard seed, and decided to forget about calling Rose. I'd run there instead; it was just up the road.

Turning fast and passing through the door, I stopped for a minute. I'd lock up, keep those thieves outside where they belonged. Fiddling with the doorknob, I groaned. There was no lock. I reckon Papaw just never saw the need for locking himself in or for locking others out. Not on Muckwater Mountain, where mountaineers are always free.

Woof-Woof. I forgot Woof-Woof. Nobody was going to take my Woof-Woof away. I whipped around again and went back in.

There he was, upside down in the middle of my bed, staring up at my Dream Dog Display. His matted old stub of a tail looked sad, as if he'd seen too much of life to want to wag.

I picked him up, searching the bed and the floor and the wardrobe. No mustard seed. No faith. Maybe everything *wouldn't* be okay after all. Maybe Papaw would never come home, maybe my money was gone forever, maybe Woof-Woof was the only dog I'd ever have. I blinked, hard, and hugged Woof-Woof warm in my arms, heading for the door.

Before leaving, I looked around once more. Everything was in place, the way Papaw and I always left Bark Shanty. There was the coffeepot on the counter and Papaw's denture cup smack-dab in the middle of the kitchen table, like a centerpiece. There was the kitchen towel tied on to the handle of the icebox and the two bath towels draped over the edge of the tub. There was Papaw's medicine on the windowsill and my books piled up beside the woodstove and Papaw's glassworking tools in a box by the old green sofa. It was funny: I always hated that sofa, but somehow now I loved the thing. It was sort of a booger-green color, with sagging old cushions of some kind of scratchy material. I stared at the sofa, thinking of how the threat of losing something made a person really appreciate that thing. If the thief took that sofa, I would really miss it, same way I'd miss the coffeepot and the denture cup and everything else in Bark Shanty. I took a deep breath and then closed my eyes, memorizing Bark Shanty and everything in it. There, now I knew it by heart, same way I knew Papaw and Mamaw and Mama and Daddy and Emmie. If you know somebody—or something—by heart, then nothing can ever take that from you. Not death, not a thief.

I hugged Woof-Woof tight to my heart. "Good-bye, Bark Shanty," I said out loud, my words flat in our empty home. "I'll be home soon, I hope, and so will Papaw." *I hope. I hope.*

"Woof-Woof," I said, holding him up so we saw eye to eye, "if you were a real dog, I'd leave you here to guard against thieves."

Woof-Woof just stared, as unreal as could be with those hard plastic eyes. I kissed him on his broken mouth, tucked him under my arm, and headed out, slamming the door behind me.

15

A Glint of Gold

"YOU WERE *what?*" Rose's eyes, wide and stupefied, bulged big and blue in the late afternoon sunlight.

"Robbed, Rose," I said, collapsing onto the Robertses' porch swing. "I was robbed. You know, when somebody takes something from you." I gulped, trying to catch my breath.

"What did they take?" Rose, standing there in her shimmery pink swimming suit, looked like a *Teen Magazine* model, all glistening and tanned, her hair shining in the sun.

I sniffed. Rose smelled like baby oil. "All my money," I said.

Rose squinted and shook her head, her dreamcatchers glinting silver. "How much did you have?" she asked.

"Enough," I said. "Enough for all the dog stuff." I swiped at my eyes.

"And my mustard-seed necklace is lost," I added.

Rose shrugged. "That thing was so ugly, anyway," she said.

I sighed. "But it belonged to Mama," I said. "It meant a lot to me."

Rose rubbed at her arms, massaging in the baby oil that she said helped to give her a tan. I reckon Rose didn't read all those magazine articles about skin cancer and such, because she just kept on baking herself like an oiled fish.

"We'll find your mustard seed," she said finally.

"Where?" I asked. "I looked everywhere, all over Bark Shanty and the yard."

Rose thought, scrunching up her forehead. "I remember you were wearing it when you got on the bus, after school," she said.

I closed my eyes, looking back in time. "I was!" I said. "I remember seeing water dripping from it after the Dud dumped water on me and woke me up."

Rose crossed her arms, all puffed-up and pleased with herself. "We'll walk up to Percy's house," she said. "It's most likely on the bus."

"And what about my money?" I asked, lifting my sweat-soaked hair from my neck. "Shouldn't we call the police or something?"

Rose bit her lip, smearing lipstick all over her teeth. "I don't know," she said, frowning. "I wish my parents were home."

Rose was always wishing her parents were home. What Papaw called highfalutin high-paid professional folks, Rose's mother and father spent all their time making money. I reckon that's the price folks pay for being house people: wasting all the sunshine while they sit in an office earning the mortgage payment.

"We do need to call the police," I decided, "but first, let's find my mustard seed."

We went into the air-conditioned kitchen, and Rose ran upstairs to slip into some shorts. I sank onto one of the fancy chairs, my head spinning like the Robertses' new-fangled food processor, chopping at my thoughts and churning them all together. *My money, my mustard seed, my papaw.* I felt like a popped balloon, all deflated and flat.

Glancing at the grandfather clock ticking away in the corner. I saw that it was 4:35. *4:35!* I was supposed to be at Stonecrest Kennels at 5:00. The Queen would have a royal conniption fit if her poo-poos didn't get fed at the stroke of six.

"Rose!" I hollered up the steps. "Hurry!"

"Just a minute," floated her voice. "I'm just finishing my mascara."

Mascara! Even if the whole earth was blowing up around her, Rose Roberts would be fussing with her face. She'd go out with a smile on her lips all right, a shiny, pink, heart-shaped smile.

"Rose," I yelled. "Come on. I need to get to work."

Rose bounded down the steps, all gussied up in a salmon-colored shorts set. You'd have thought she was going to see the president or something, the way she was so dressed up.

We set off, heading up Boghill Road toward Percy's house, which was halfway between Rose's home and the Castle.

"So who do you think did it?" asked Rose.

"What?" I asked.

"Stole your money," Rose said.

"Len Ryler," I said. "I think it was Len Ryler. That boy has a rotten look in his eyes." I bit the insides of my cheeks to keep from laughing.

"Silver!" Rose squealed. "I'm serious." Just the mention of Len Ryler's name brought a blush to her cheeks, a blush that couldn't be bought in Kmart.

I scowled, trying to look serious. "I don't know, Rose. It could have been just about anybody." I cast her a sideways glance. "It could have been *you*."

"Silver Nickles!" hissed Rose. "Do you really think I'd do such a thing?"

"Nah," I said. "The only thing you'd ever steal is somebody else's boyfriend." I grinned, thinking I was pretty clever.

Rose rolled her eyes, and we kept walking in silence for a few minutes. I could smell Rose's perfume cooking away in the June light, something flowery and sweet.

"Maybe it was that Avon lady," Rose said, right out of the blue.

"What?" I asked.

"That Avon lady who keeps pestering your papaw to buy something," she said. "Maybe she snitched your money."

"Rose," I said, "that Avon lady is too busy bugging people to have time to go around stealing money from coffee cans. And anyway, she has honest eyes, underneath all that makeup."

"Maybe it was that face," Rose said, one pointed fingernail on her chin.

"What face?" I snapped. Rose was making

less and less sense the closer to thirteen she got. Her birthday was a week before mine.

"That face at my window," she said. "That man in the woods last night."

"I thought you didn't believe that," I said, stopping. We were almost at Percy's driveway.

"I didn't," said Rose. "But now I do."

I shuddered, thinking of the man in the trees and the face in the window. "I don't know," I said, goose bumps prickling my arms.

"Or," said Rose, as we turned into Percy's long, curved driveway, "it could have been the Dud. Or the Dud's dad."

"The Dud's dad?" I asked. "I've never even seen him."

"Exactly," said Rose, smacking her fist against her palm. "That makes him a prime suspect."

"While we're at it," I said, eyeing the banana-yellow bus hulking at the top of the hill, "we may as well accuse the Queen and Pastor Pete."

"Hey," said Rose, "I didn't even think of them."

I just shook my head, gazing at old Number 36. *My mustard seed. Please, please, please.* I crossed all my fingers, even though I *really* didn't believe in such stuff. We were getting closer and closer, and my heart began to thump.

"Hi, girls," called Percy, who was watering his flower garden. "Miss me already?" Percy was the nicest man, all rosy-cheeked and white-whiskered, like a skinny old Santa Claus.

"Hi, Percy," I said, nervous. "I lost my necklace on the way home. May we look on the bus?" I picked at my fingernails.

"Sure!" said Percy, nodding and smiling like Santa granting a wish.

Rose and I looked at each other, and then we pushed open the creaky old bus door. It smelled damp and musty inside, like a mildewed basement room. Some of the seats were still wet, and there was a mess of trash on the floor, stuff like spitballs and paper airplanes and candy wrappers and failed tests. Poor Percy, stuck with cleaning up all the mess of the last day of school.

I stood on the top step, heavy with that weird feeling of going back to the place I was just before something happened. When I'd last stood on these steps, I'd had no idea that I would lose my money and my mustard seed.

Rose poked at me from behind. "Go on, Silver," she said. "You'll never find your necklace, standing there daydreaming."

I took a deep breath, and then a step, looking left and right and down and all around, hoping to see the golden chain shining from the mess. I took another step, and then another, slow steps as I sifted through the trash on the floor.

"There it is!" Rose shouted over my shoulder.

I stopped, my heart caught in my throat. "Where?" I breathed.

"Right there." Rose pointed with a curved pink fingernail, and I looked down. Flashing from the mess on the floor was a glint of gold, gleaming bright and shiny below my eyes.

"Thank you," I sighed, bending down and reaching into the litter.

It was a candy wrapper, a cellophane candy wrapper shimmering gold and shiny in my hands.

16

Looking High and Low

"WHERE ELSE COULD IT BE?" I asked as we traipsed down Percy's driveway.

Rose shrugged, and then her eyes lit up. She grinned. "Think, Silver," she said, and smacked my arm. "You were wearing it when you got on the bus, right?"

I nodded.

"So where else did you go, besides the bus and Bark Shanty?" she asked, talking in a tone she'd use with a two-year-old.

I just shrugged, not appreciating Rose's tone of voice. I hated being babied.

Rose nudged me in the ribs. "You went to Mud Creek," she said with a wink. "And hugged the Dud."

"I did not!" I said. "*He* hugged *me*."

"Silver," said Rose, "that's beside the point. *You went to Mud Creek.* That's where your necklace is."

I looked at her and then grabbed Rose for a hug, not even caring if I got lipstick on my shoulder. It was Rose's shirt anyway, and not my style. I hated puffy sleeves and lace.

"Rose Roberts," I said, "you're a genius."

"I know," said Rose as we turned onto Boghill Road.

"And you're modest, too," I said, breaking into a run. Rose's shorts, a little too baggy for me, flapped around my legs.

Rose followed, and we headed through the woods toward the creek. Jogging along, I imagined my necklace dangling just ahead, like a fishing worm on a hook. Through the trees, past the old dump where Muckwater Mountain used to discard its garbage, around the bend . . . and there it was. Mud Creek, mucky, slow, and brown. I jumped up and down; Mud Creek had never looked so good.

"Now, where were you and your boyfriend hugging?" Rose asked, panting from the run.

I punched her arm. "The Dud is not my boyfriend," I said, heading for the bank of the creek. "He was hiding here." I ran my hand across the trunk of a tree shaped like a **V**, checking the ground around the tree.

"No," I said, looking up. "It was *this* tree." I moved to a smaller, skinnier tree.

"*Sil-ver*," wailed Rose. "We'll never find your necklace this way."

"This is the tree," I said, nodding. "I remember the carved hearts." I traced the outline of the intertwined hearts etched in the bark.

"*D* and *S*," Rose shrieked, reading the initials carved in the middle of each heart. "Silver and the Dud!"

"Rose," I said, teeth clenched.

"Well, who else could it be?" Rose smirked.

I ignored her, looking high and low for my necklace. It was nowhere near the tree, so I moved slowly toward the creek, scanning the ground. Rose joined me, and together we paced the bank of Mud Creek, finding nothing.

"It must be in the water," I said, sitting on a rock to take off my shoes. They smelled damp and musty, like the school bus, and were still wet from the water fight earlier in the day. I tossed my shoes to the side and waded into the mucky brown water.

Shivering, I trudged through the water,

peering into the muck. Sunshine filtered through the trees, making patterns of circles and diamonds and squares that danced before me on the surface of the water. I closed my eyes for a second and then looked again, moving up the creek a bit. My feet were numb, all mired in the cold mud.

"Would it float or sink?" Rose called. She was perched on the rock, legs crossed prissily.

"I don't know," I said. "Sink, I reckon. It's pretty heavy."

"Then you should be raking the bottom with your hands," Rose pronounced. Little Miss Priss, sitting there in her makeup and jewelry and salmon-colored shorts set, acting as though she'd dissolve if she got wet.

I took a breath and reached deep into the swampy stuff at the bottom, oozing the muck through my fingers. When I was little, Daddy told me that Mud Creek was made of quicksand and that I'd sink clear to Swampville if I ever dared to step into the creek.

I looked down, seeing that I was getting a mud hem on Rose's silky pink shorts, and dug deeper into the glop. Something slimy squirmed beneath my fingers and I screamed, squishing backward through the scummy water. A snake squiggled off across the creek, heading for the bank. I screamed again, staring at the dark and wiggly thing worming its way through the water.

"Silver, what on earth?" Rose was standing, hands on hips, and scowling. She looked like a schoolteacher who had just sat on a tack or got zinged with a rubber band.

"A snake!" I shrieked, cringing. *"I touched a snake!"* I swished my hands fast through the top of the water, wincing. I felt all fidgety, as if snakes were squirming all over my body.

"Do you want to find your necklace or don't you?" demanded Little Miss Priss Schoolteacher, hands still on her hips.

"'Do you want to find your necklace or don't you?'" I mocked, giving it one last shot and skimming the bottom.

Nothing. I sloshed from the water and snatched my shoes, sitting on the rock and muttering to myself as I yanked a shoe over my muddy foot. "With luck like this, I'll be an old lady before I ever get a dog," I mumbled. "Maybe more like *thirty*, instead of *thirteen*."

"What?" Rose called from the side of the creek, peering into the muck as if she could bring my necklace to the surface with her stare.

"Nothing, Rose. Nothing." I picked up my other shoe and threw it hard, aiming at the carved hearts on the tree. It missed the tree and landed with a smack in Mud Creek.

Rose swiveled her stare and fixed it on me. "Now, Silver," she said, common sense oozing from her voice. "Throwing your shoe into the creek does no good. You said yourself, all it takes is faith, and hard work, and . . ."

Work! I was supposed to be at Stonecrest Kennels at 5:00 and it must be past five by now! I leaped up and dashed into the woods, slogging along in one wet shoe.

"Silver," shouted Rose, "what are you doing?"

"Going to work," I yelled, not looking back. "Today's a Monday, remember?"

Rose ran up behind me. "The Queen would give you a vacation day for the last day of school," she said.

I stopped, yanking off my shoe and throwing it down by Rose. "I need the money more than ever," I said. "I *have* to go to work today." And then I lit off, barefoot, up Boghill Road. The Castle was less than a half mile away, but it took about twenty minutes to get there, on account of all the twists and turns and hills.

"Silver!" shouted Rose.

I turned. Rose was standing in the middle of the road, holding my shoe like a stop sign.

"What should I do with this?" she asked.

"Throw it away," I said.

Rose pouted. "But *my* shoes won't fit you," she said.

I shrugged. "So I'll buy new shoes," I said. "That's another reason to get to work." I waved and took off, my feet smarting from hot tar and gravel.

Up, up, up, around, turn, up, up, up, around, down . . . and I was there. The Castle. I flopped onto a rock and examined the soles of my feet. They were raw and red and sore, and as I sat there rubbing them, I wished that I could examine my *soul* the way I examined my soles. I had a funny feeling that my soul might be every bit as raw and red and sore, if only I could see it.

I looked out across the driveway at the Castle. So stone-cold and silent, it always looked empty, as if nobody lived there.

I took a deep breath and then headed for the kennels, wondering what time it was. My stomach was growling, and I wished I'd grabbed a sandwich at Rose's before running on up.

Smoothing down my hair and straightening my shirt, I approached the big, black door of the purple bruise and rang the bell, that stupid yip-yap bell of the Queen's.

The door swung open, and there stood the Queen, her eyes crisscrossed with streaks of red.

"6:16," she snapped, whipping up her wrist and glaring at her purple watch.

"I'm sorry," I said, shifting from foot to foot, "but I've had lots of trouble, you see. Somebody robbed the money I'd been saving to buy a dog and I lost this necklace that used to belong to my mother and then I was looking in the creek for the necklace and I lost my shoe, so I had to run here barefoot."

The Queen looked down at me, taking in everything from my dirty feet to the mud-caked shorts to the rumpled shirt to my sweaty hair.

"He's dead," she said. "And you're fired."

17

Some Mighty Strange Things on Muckwater Mountain

"So SHE BLAMED YOU for the death of the Little Prince?" Rose asked, sitting at her vanity and fussing with her hair.

I nodded, miserable. "I can't believe she would think such a thing," I said, flopping down on the bed. "I wouldn't hurt a *flea*, let alone one of her doggone prize poodles."

"Prize?" asked Rose, turning to look at me.

"She takes them to dog shows and such," I said, picking at my nails. "Wins lots of fancy blue ribbons and trophies to decorate the kennels."

"Well, there's the answer," Rose said, slapping her hand down on her knee.

"Where?" I asked, staring at Rose's well-oiled knee.

"Prize poodles," Rose said, raising her plucked eyebrows. "Big bucks. Worth their weight in gold. Somebody poisoned the Little Prince."

"Rose," I said, rolling my eyes. "Why on earth would somebody do that?"

"To get rid of the competition," Rose said, so sure of herself that she practically crowed. Inspector Rose Roberts, dog detective.

"Well," I said, counting on my fingers, "for one thing, the Queen always keeps the kennels locked. Number two: why would they choose the Little Prince? There's a whole passel of dogs in that place. Why wouldn't they just kill or steal the whole kit and caboodle, while they were in there? Number three: we don't even know that the Little Prince was poisoned. He could have just had some doggie disease or something. He was such a runt, *anything* could have happened." I sighed.

Rose shrugged. "It was just an idea," she said, all offended and mopey.

I gazed at the white canopy. "Some mighty strange things are happening lately on Muckwater Mountain," I said.

Rose finished twisting her hair into a braid. "I still say it was that face," she said. "That man in the woods."

"What man?" It was Mrs. Roberts, poking her face into the doorway of Rose's room.

"Mom!" Rose jumped up and grabbed her mother in a hug. "I didn't know you were home from work!"

Mrs. Roberts kissed Rose on the cheek and then clicked off in her blue high heels and business suit, looking distracted.

I sighed, dreading another sleepless night at Rose's house. "I wish Papaw was coming home," I said, standing up and looking through the window. The sun was setting behind the mountain, a big ball of orange and pink, like a wet jawbreaker candy.

"Oh!" said Rose, slapping her head. "I forgot! Pastor Pete called while you were gone. He's taking you to the hospital tomorrow morning to pick up your papaw and bring him home."

My heart leaped, then set like the sun. "Did you tell Pastor Pete about the money and my mustard seed?" I asked, hoping that Pastor Pete was on prayer duty for me right that very minute.

"No," Rose said. "I figured that was up to you to do."

I sighed, running my hand through my matted hair. I felt as though all the happenings

116

of the day were tangled up in my hair: the hug from the Dud, the water battle, the missing money and mustard seed, my lost shoe, getting fired at Stonecrest Kennels, and accused of a crime to boot. What a horrible, rotten, no-good kind of day. No wonder that old song said something about Mondays being so bad.

"I reckon I'll hop in the shower," I said to Rose. "Wash away the day."

Rose ignored me, caking more makeup on her eyes. "I wonder if I'll see Len Ryler this summer?" she asked her reflection in the funhouse mirror.

I snorted. All Rose cared about was boys. Boys and makeup and her figure. I never even looked at my figure, let alone fretted about it the way Rose did. She was always talking about going on some stupid diet or exercise program, when she looked just fine the way she was. I never could figure out why some folks fussed about their outsides so much, when that was the part that would just die someday anyway.

I dragged down the hallway toward Rose's bathroom. The Robertses had two bathrooms, one for Rose and one for her parents. Rose's room was all pink, of course: pink toilet, tub, sink, curtains, rug, and tile on the wall. Rose even had pink toilet paper, for heaven's sake.

Going into the bathroom and slamming shut the door, I turned on Rose's shower radio. Some guy was singing about faith, believe it or not, something about how you gotta have faith. I changed the station, wondering what on earth that Hollywood rock and roller thought he knew about faith. Bet he had more money than faith, any day.

I stripped down and tossed my dirty clothes in the pink laundry hamper. Every night Rose's mother emptied that hamper, tossed the laundry in her shiny white Maytag, folded the clean clothes, and stacked them on Rose's bed. At home, I was the one who ended up doing the laundry . . . both mine and Papaw's, in the old wringer washing machine.

I unhooked my bra and examined it for dirt, noticing how there was still an outline of the durnfool blue flower I cut off months ago. Draping my bra over the edge of the hamper, I climbed into the shower and turned on the water. Hot water, as hot as my skin could stand. I loved showers; they felt so much cleaner and quicker than baths.

Standing there under the steamy spray and lathering away, I kept thinking of how the Dud grabbed me and hugged me. Even though I *despised* the Dud, having been hugged by a boy made me feel different somehow. More grownup, womanly. I looked down, but my body hadn't changed. It was still as stick-straight and skinny as a fence post, all skin and bones, as Papaw said.

I rinsed my hair until it squeaked, which made me think of the Little Prince. Tears brimmed in my eyes, but I washed them down the drain, determined not to let the Queen get the better of me. Hopefully, I'd get a good night's sleep and nothing would seem so bad tomorrow. That had happened before, when things seemed impossible, and the changing of the days made things okay somehow.

Turning off the water and drying with the fluffy pink towel, I decided to go to bed real early. A clean cotton nightgown hung on the back of the door, and I slipped into it, after wrestling back into my bra.

Woof-Woof, I thought. I'd forgotten all about Woof-Woof, out on the porch swing. I'd tossed him there before Rose and I left to look for my mustard seed, down at the creek.

Yanking a comb through my hair, I walked through the hallway, down the stairs, and outside, into the growing dark. There was a slight breeze, which made me shiver, and the swing was moving slowly, creaking. It was eerie: the empty driveway and the dark house and the swing swaying in the wind. I groped through the dusk, reaching for Woof-Woof.

My hand mets nothing by wood, cool and smooth. Woof-Woof was gone!

18

A Brand-Spankin' New Day

WOOF-WOOF WAS MISSING. That was the last straw; I had all the burdens I could bear. One more would break me for sure.

I went to bed and bawled my eyes out, hoping that Rose wouldn't hear from the television room downstairs. I bawled for my mustard seed, I bawled for my money, I bawled for the Little Prince. I bawled for the Dud's glasses and for my job at Stonecrest Kennels and for Woof-Woof. I bawled for Mama and Daddy and Emmie and Mamaw and Papaw and myself. I bawled for a dog, wishing that my Dream Dog Display hung above my head.

I'd never have my dream dog by July, not at this rate. Too many things were going wrong. I felt heavy and bloated, all weighed down and filled up with problems. Wiping my eyes, I drifted off to sleep, away from the soggy sorrow of real life. It almost felt like floating out of my body, drifting off so slow and sad.

It was morning. Sunlight poured like maple syrup into the bedroom, spilling all over Rose and me. I stretched and yawned, and then remembered. *Today is the day!* Papaw was coming home. Papaw was coming home, and everything would be all right. I smiled, rubbing my eyes, and rolled out of bed with a thump. Rose didn't budge; she was sleeping as snug as a bug in a rug.

I went downstairs to the kitchen and poured a glass of orange juice, the expensive kind thick with hunks of pulp. The kitchen was quiet and clean; Rose's parents were gone. They were always gone, it seemed. I'd never realized until the past week how often Rose was alone.

Downing the juice and a cheese pastry, I stuck the cup in the dishwasher. The Robertses had all kinds of machines to do the work: a dishwasher, a riding mower, a remote control for the television, an electric can opener, an ice maker on the fridge, an electric ice-cream maker. I reckoned that's how some folks got fat, what with all those lazy-making machines. I kind of liked the feeling of doing things by hand.

Meandering out onto the front porch, I took a deep breath of the fresh morning air. Summer vacation air. I loved that smell: no school bus fumes or teacher's perfume to stink up the days—just glistening green mountain air, best in the early morning when birds chirped and dew-diamond drops glittered on the grass.

Standing there on the fancy porch in one of Rose's prissy white nightgowns, I faced the mountains around me and swore not to lose faith. I'd just start over, that's all. Today was a brand-spankin' new day . . . the first day of the rest of my life, as they say. I may not have my job or my money or my mustard seed or my Woof-Woof, but I'd get my dream dog. By my birthday, too . . . or my name wasn't Silver Iris Nickles. *If ye have faith as a grain of mustard seed, ye shall say unto this mountain, Remove hence to yonder place; and it shall remove; and nothing shall be impossible unto you.*

"Remove hence to yonder place," I shouted at the mountain, and then grinned and went back into the house. Snatching up the cordless telephone from the counter, I moseyed back outside and punched in the hospital number. That number felt like part of me, after seven days of calling Papaw morning and night.

"Room 213," I told the lady at the desk, who always sounded stuffed up and miserable. I reckon that's what working in a place where people are sick and hurt does to you.

Without a word, the lady put me through to Papaw's room, connected us across the miles just like the snap of a finger. *Thank God for telephones*, I thought, imagining how awful it would be not to hear Papaw's voice every day.

The phone rang and rang, and my heart quickened, wondering what was taking Papaw so long. He usually picked up on the second ring, regular as clockwork. *What if he died?* I pictured that cold white bed, all made up and empty and smelling like Lysol.

Come on, Papaw. Answer your phone. Please. . . It rang and rang, shrilling and pleading to the empty room. I felt sick to my stomach, all full of puke and sorrow and worry. Where was Papaw? It didn't take *that* long to get across the room and pick up the phone, for heaven's sake.

I pushed the Off button, then Redial. "Are you sure you gave me Room 213?" I demanded of Mrs. Stuffed-Up and Miserable.

"Room 213," repeated the lady, all fast and huffylike, and the phone rang again. And again and again and again. I sank onto the porch swing, counting the rings. On ring number eighteen, I hung up.

My head was spinning, and I felt all weak and shaky. *Where was Papaw?* I closed my eyes and pictured him, all bright-eyed and bushy-tailed and ready to get the heck out of there.

"Good morning, Silver." My eyes flew open to the sight of Pastor Pete, bouncing along like a skinny little elf, all dressed in light green.

"Good . . . good morning," I stuttered, stunned. I was mortified to have Pastor Pete see me in a *nightgown*, sitting on the front porch as though I owned the place. "I'll run in and get dressed," I said. "Be right back." I dashed inside and then remembered my manners. It wasn't very polite to leave the preacher all alone on the porch like that, standing there as if his feet were too dirty to go inside.

I opened the door and popped my head outside. Just my head. "Come on in and wait in the kitchen, Pastor Pete," I said. "Rose's parents left some coffee on." Then I lit off up the steps, almost ripping out the bottom of Rose's nightgown by taking them three at a time.

"Rose," I hissed, shaking her. "Wake up. Pastor Pete is here."

"Len?" muttered Rose, rolling over. She looked like a raccoon in the mornings, what with that black mascara smudged up underneath her eyes.

"No, it's not Len," I snapped, yanking her pillow out from beneath her head. Just pulled her heart right out from under her.

Rose sat up, all dumbfounded. "What are you doing, Silver?" Rose Roberts and her stupid questions. She was beginning to work on my nerves, after more than a week of those confounded questions.

"What does it look like I'm doing?" I asked, sarcastic, standing there in my bra and underpants. "I'm getting dressed."

"What do you need me for?" Rose asked, picking makeup from the corners of her eyes. Most folks had sleepymen in the mornings; Rose had dried-up globs of eye shadow.

"I need you to find me an outfit," I said, spacing out my words the way Rose spaced out her perfume, dotting it in a line up and down her inner arm.

Rose sighed and dragged herself from the bed, yanking open the top drawer of her white bureau. That bureau was no-man's-land; nobody touched it but Rose Roberts.

"There," she said, thrusting a sissified little jumpsuit in my face. It was all frilly and flouncy, white, with a hem of rickrack ruffly stuff fringing the bottom. I'd look like a walking bedroom curtain.

Mumbling to myself, I tugged on the outfit, hitching it up around my waist. Grabbing Rose's comb, I worked the rats from my hair, pulling out a couple of clumps in the process.

Making a beeline for the staircase, I glanced down at the prissy outfit I couldn't believe I was wearing. And then I remembered: I had no shoes.

19

Clara Cough Cough Cooper

Flip-flopping DOWN THE hospital hallway in Rose's mother's sandals, I felt my heart slapping around like the shoes. What if Pastor Pete and I were greeted with an empty bed and the smell of Lysol?

Closer and closer to Papaw's room, we moved. Room 201, 202, 203, 204 . . . I knew from somewhere deep and scary inside of me that if Papaw died I'd cry until kingdom come, at the top of my lungs. I'd wail and sob and scream so loud that all of Swampville would hear me, even those folks on Main Street, living in my old house.

210, 211 . . . I hadn't told Pastor Pete about trying to call Papaw this morning, maybe because if I put it into words, it would make it real.

212. *Please*, I prayed.

213. Even before going into the room, I smelled the Lysol. I rubbed my nose, wanting to make the smell go away. Then I followed Pastor Pete into the room, almost closing my eyes. The bed was empty, the sheets neat and new and crisply in place. The curtains were drawn down the middle of the room, and Papaw's glasses were gone. So was the hospital cup he used to clean his dentures. And the *Stained Glassworkers* magazine I brought him on Sunday, the last time I saw him.

Everything in my body seemed to stop: my breath, my heart, my blood, my bones. "Papaw," I said, inside. My lips didn't move, and no sound came out.

"Well," said Pastor Pete, flipping on the television. "We'll just wait here for Brother Walt." He didn't even realize what must have happened.

"You'll have a mighty long wait." The sharp voice cut through the heavy curtains, lodging in my heart like a sliver of glass. *A forever wait*, I thought, sick.

Pastor Pete grinned and walked over to the curtains, pulling them back as though somebody had died and left him boss.

"Walter went for tests," said the voice, and relief flooded me, almost knocking me over like a big wave at the ocean.

"Tests, tests, and more tests," whined the voice. "Those eternal tests. If the heart attack doesn't kill you, the tests will."

It was a lady, an old lady, with a fluff of pure white hair and a pink face creased with lines. She put me in mind of a wilted carnation thrown out in a pile of snow.

Pastor Pete bounded over to the bed and shook her hand. "Pete Parnell, ma'am," he said, pumping her hand as if it were one of those old-fashioned gasoline pumps down at the Swampville Sunoco station.

"Clara Cooper," coughed the lady. It was like, Clara—Cough, Cough—Cooper.

"And this is Brother Walt's granddaughter, Silver," said Pastor Pete, waving his arms with a flourish, as if I were a prize package on *The Price Is Right*.

"Clara (cough, cough) Cooper," said the lady again, holding out a tiny blue-veined hand. I shook it, thinking it felt like bird claws.

Clara Cough Cough Cooper was looking at me with bright blue eyes sunken into her pink face like two slits of the sky. Her eyes were red-rimmed like an old beagle dog, and as steady as steel. She stared and stared, still holding my hand, and then blinked hard and long. Her eyelids were thin and pale and blue-veined like her hands.

"You're the spittin' image of my best friend from the year 1937," said Clara Cough Cough Cooper, slowly opening her eyes. "Hallie Jacobs. She drowned."

Oh, wonderful, I thought, wishing she'd let go of my hand. *Thank you for sharing that.*

"You were here on Sunday, weren't you?" Clara Cough Cough Cooper fixed those eyes on me again.

I nodded.

Clara Cough Cough Cooper dropped my hand and twisted a pearl ball balancing on her pink ear. The earring looked enormous, like a scoop of vanilla ice cream topping a strawberry. A dried-out, withered-up old strawberry.

"Your grandfather is a fine man," said Clara Cough Cough Cooper, still turning that earring around and around. Maybe it was the volume to a hearing aid or something. "I was hoping he'd introduce us on Sunday, but the old fool's a tad bashful."

Just then, Papaw shuffled into the room, grexing and complaining to the nurses bringing up the rear. But as soon as he saw us, his eyes lit up. Sunshine on swamp soil.

"Silver!" he said, his raspy voice all full of love. And then he hugged me, for the first time in a coon's age.

"And Pete," Papaw said, backing away from me and inching toward Pastor Pete for a handshake.

"Why are you walking so funny, Papaw?" I asked.

Papaw pointed at the blue-striped hospital gown fluttering around his knees. "This thing opens in the back," he grumbled, taking itty-bitty baby steps toward Pastor Pete and grasping the back of his gown.

I snickered, thinking how I never thought I'd see the day when Papaw would sport a *dress*, especially one that gaped open in the behind.

"Pastor Pete." Papaw nodded, trying to act all tough and manly and seriouslike, even though he was dressed in something about as sissified as the bedroom curtain I wore.

"*Pastor* Pete!" yowled Clara Cough Cough Cooper. "This is the fellow you were talking about, Walter?"

Papaw grinned and ducked his head, almost blushing. "This is the fella," he said.

"Pastor Pete," announced Clara Cough Cough Cooper, "is going to marry us."

A Soul Must Do
What a Soul Must Do

"ARE YOU AND THAT LADY really getting married?" I asked Papaw the minute Pastor Pete dropped us off at Bark Shanty. We were still in the yard, making our way through shin-tickling grass and weeds. Papaw was back in his old soldier's uniform, just as though it was still Memorial Day and nothing had ever happened.

"Yep," Papaw said, sifting through a hog's mess of mail he'd pulled from the mailbox. "Gettin' hitched."

"Well," I said, stomping along in my white bedroom curtain. "If you can get a wife, I can get a dog."

"Silver," growled Papaw. "You'll get a dog over my . . ."

"Don't even say it, Papaw," I cut in, yanking

open the door. There it was: Bark Shanty, with everything just the way I'd left it yesterday. There was the coffeepot on the counter and Papaw's denture cup smack-dab in the middle of the kitchen table. There was the kitchen towel tied onto the icebox and the two bath towels draped over the edge of the tub. (How would we ever fit *three* towels on there, if Clara Cough Cough Cooper became Papaw's wife?) There was Papaw's medicine on the windowsill and my books piled up beside the woodstove and Papaw's glassworking tools in a box by the old green sofa.

"Home, sweet home," I said. Bark Shanty answered: *Welcome.* The cat clock ticked and the icebox hummed, greeting us with their old familiar sounds. I thought how funny it was that those noises went on the whole week we were gone, even though nobody was there to hear them. Except the *thief.*

"Papaw," I said, taking his elbow, "you'd better sit down a spell. I have some things to tell you." I hadn't broken the news of all my problems during the ride home from the hospital, because I wanted that to be a happy and joyful time, as bright as Pastor Pete's little red car. Home was the place for problems, and now was the time to tell Papaw of all that had happened while he was gone.

Papaw lowered himself slowly onto the sofa, and I noticed that his uniform wasn't quite so tight as it had been a week ago. He'd lost weight in the hospital, along with the color in his cheeks. Well, I'd have him up to par within a week, all fattened up and rosy-cheeked.

I sat down beside him, on the old booger-green sofa, and felt safer and more secure than I'd felt all week in the Robertses' fancy house.

Papaw reached out and took my hand. "First," he said, "*I* have some things to tell *you*."

He took a deep breath. "I love Miss Clara with all the heart I have left," he said, thumping his chest. The Purple Heart swung, and Papaw continued. "When they put her on the other side of that curtain, the day after my heart attack, we talked a tin ear, just as if we'd known each other all our lives. Gabbed and gabbed and gabbed, all day long, spillin' the beans about the years past and times to come. Couldn't even see the little lady, but by the next day, I knew I loved her." He smiled gently, his rock-hard face softening.

"How could you love somebody after just one day?" I asked, standing up and opening the window above the sink. It was getting downright stuffy in there.

"Silver," said Papaw, as I sat back down beside him, "when you're as old as me, you don't have forever to fall in love. If you're going to do it, you'd best do it fast, because there's not that much time to waste. A soul must do what a soul must do."

"And you must marry her," I said sulkily. I picked at my fingernails.

"I must marry her," Papaw said, "to feel whole again. I've been livin' all these years with half a heart, Silver, ever since Mamaw passed on. Then, in the blink of an eye, that durnfool heart attack stole right in and tried to strike away the other half. Miss Clara gave me back my heart."

I looked him straight in the eyes. "But what about Mamaw?" I asked.

Papaw took my hand again. "Silver," he said, "Mamaw is dancin' the jig in Paradise right now, because she knows this old geezer will be happy once more. That's all she ever wanted, was for me to be happy. And, you know, I'll never stop loving Mamaw. I always have and I always will be so in love with that gal that I can't see straight." He took off his glasses and polished them on the tail of his shirt, then laid them on the arm of the sofa. He looked raw and open without his glasses.

"I just now got it through my head why I've been fightin' against you gettin' a hound dog, Silver," he said, running his hands through his fuzzy white hair and closing his eyes for a moment.

"Why?" I asked. *No room in Bark Shanty for a dog. Why, there's barely enough room for an old man and a twelve-year-old girl.* I wondered how we'd ever find room for Clara Cough Cough Cooper.

"The reason I've been fightin' it," said Papaw, "is on account of an old, old memory buried deep in my mind. From back when your mama was just your age, twelve goin' on thirteen, and just as pretty as could be. Just like you. Wheat-colored hair and those twinklin' brown eyes, toppin' off a body skinny as the edge of the moon." He smiled sadly and looked at me.

"You and your mama were cut from the same cloth," he said. "Pretty as a picture and bullheaded as all get-out. Well, that winter your mama was twelve, we went and got her a dog. Frisky little huntin' dog, with a tail that wagged to beat the band and legs that ran like the wind. We named her Blue, on account of a tiny little blue spot smack-dab in the middle of her back. Never saw anything like it. Well, your mama was crazy about old Blue, so crazy she couldn't see anything else. Everything was Blue, Blue, Blue. Slept with Blue, ate with Blue at her feet, even caught her takin' a bath with Blue one time."

I smiled and closed my eyes, trying to picture my mama and Blue, all those years ago before I even existed.

"Well," said Papaw, his voice shaky and slow, "came a springtime day when Blue got herself run over by the milk truck. Just ran right out and under those big old tires, in plain sight of your mama." He shook his head.

"I thought she'd never stop grieving," Papaw said. "Cried when she went to bed, cried when she ate supper, cried when she took a bath. Cried every time she saw another dog or a milk truck or that exact shade of blue. Cried whenever one of Mamaw's cats brushed against her leg, wishin' it was Blue. Seemed like she'd never get over it, grieving for that dog." Papaw's eyes were watery.

"Durn near tore me to pieces, seeing my little

girl hurting so bad," Papaw said. "Got so I cussed the day we ever brought that hound home, wishin' I could just go back in time and change things. I'd have given anything to keep your mama from such pain. Seemed to me that having that dog for a little while and then losing it was worse than never having it at all. The day we buried Blue, back in the garden, I thought we buried your mama's heart right along with the dog. She cried herself sick, so she did, went to bed while the sun was still shinin' and mourned that hound all through the night. Mamaw and I took turns goin' in to check on her, with Mamaw sayin' all that stuff about how it's better to have loved and lost than never to have loved at all. I thought that was all a bunch of hogwash, back then. Reckon I still thought that way, up until last week, when I came to my senses in Swampville Hospital."

Papaw started to cry, his eyes like chips of broken glass. "When Mamaw passed on," he said, "I thought my life was over. I mourned her like your mama mourned Blue, on and on. Seemed everything reminded me of her, and I got so I wished I never even loved her. Same way when we lost your mama, and your daddy, and little Emmie. I almost wished I never even loved, because the losin' hurt so bad."

I started to sob, my head on Papaw's shoulder.

"But you know what?" Papaw said. "Miss Clara made me see the light, with her voice coming like sunshine through that curtain, goin' on and on about her Samuel and all those happy years before he passed on. Then I started tellin' her about Mamaw and all *our* years, and the next thing you know, something heavy and dark lifted from my heart and floated away. It was then, at that moment, that I knew Mamaw was right. Durned if it isn't better to love and lose than never to love at all." Papaw pulled out his hankie and wiped his eyes, and then dabbed at mine.

"Silver," he said, "come your birthday, you can get your dog."

To Make a Long Story Short

I HUGGED PAPAW, dripping tears and snot all over the shoulder of his uniform. "Thank you, Papaw," I said. "Thank you for telling me all that."

"Now," said Papaw, putting his glasses back on, "what did you want to tell me?"

I picked at my fingernails. "To make a long story short," I said, "I lost my mustard seed, I lost my job, I lost my shoes, I lost Woof-Woof, somebody stole my money, and I was accused of killing a dog.

"And," I said, flopping down on the other end of the sofa, "I broke the Dud's goofy black glasses."

Papaw snorted. "Why'd you go and do that?" he asked, looking up at the ceiling. The room was getting darker and darker, and rain had begun to skitter across the roof.

"It's a long story, Papaw," I said, leaning back my head and squeezing shut my eyes, trying to squish out the memory of the Dud's hug.

"Well," said Papaw, pulling himself up off the sofa, "we'll get you another necklace, we'll get you another job, we'll get you new shoes and another musical dog, your money's in the bank, and accusations don't mean a thing, as long as you know the truth in your own heart."

"My money's in the bank?" I repeated, stunned.

Papaw nodded. "I took it from that durn-fool coffee can the Saturday before Memorial Day and opened an account for you," he said. "Keeping cash in a coffee can is about as safe as puttin' all your hopes in one place. And," Papaw added, shuffling to the kitchen and twisting open his medicine bottle, "this way it'll earn some interest for you."

I jumped up and hugged him. "Thank you, Papaw," I said, one worry lighter.

"And now," I said, looking through the window at the brightening sky, "I'm going to go change out of this bedroom curtain into some *real* clothes."

I skipped to my room, whistling away like a bird set free from a cage. There it was: my room. The stained-glass window, the little rolltop desk, Mamaw's old wardrobe in the corner, my Dream Dog Display. And finally, I'd have my dog. I wouldn't trade this for all the canopy beds on earth, I thought, sinking down on my soft and saggy bed.

And then I saw Woof-Woof at the foot of my bed, wearing the mustard seed around his tattered neck.

Dear Silver Nickles

STUCK IN WOOF-WOOF'S MOUTH was a piece of purple paper, all folded up in a neat little square. I unfolded it and saw rows of ink-black poodles, marching across the edges of the paper and hemming in the Dud's babyish handwriting. The Dud printed big and sloppy, like a second-grader.

Sitting cross-legged on my bed, cradling Woof-Woof on my lap, I read:

> Dear Silver Nickles,
> I was sorry to hear from my mother that you were fired from your job, and I wanted to let you know that the Little Prince did not die because of you. The veterinarian was here last night and said that there was

something wrong inside of him that nobody knew. Mother said that you were all full of excuses about being late, stuff like losing a necklace and looking for it in the creek, and that she could just tell you were lying. She said she knew you were no good from the moment she met you.

I hate my mother, Silver. I hate her even more than you hate science class, believe it or not. When she said that about you, I ran off down the road because I just couldn't take it anymore. I couldn't take her meanness, and I couldn't take the way she talks to me in that cold tone of voice and then turns around and makes baby talk to her stupid dogs. So I just ran and ran and, next thing you know, there I was at Rose's house.

I have to tell you something bad, Silver, and you can hate me if you want. I've been spying on you. I peeked in Rose's bedroom window when you were in there, and on Sunday night I was in her yard really late at night, trying to see if you were still awake. I was there because I was mad at my mother.

The face at the window . . . the man in the woods! It wasn't a man after all, just scrawny old Dud. I flipped over the purple paper, which smelled like the Queen, and continued to read. Now the printing was all tiny and squeezed together, as if the Dud still had a lot to say.

I even tried spying on you through your stained-glass window, but I couldn't see. I've been spying on you since the day we met, back on Easter Sunday when you were wearing that green dress. I like how you look in that dress, all tall and sparkly and bright.

Anyway, I was at Rose's again last night, trying to spy, when I saw your stuffed dog on the porch swing. (I knew it was yours, because I spied in your room once, when nobody was home.) Well, I took your dog, Silver. I took it off the swing and I took it on home, and I slept with it on my pillow beside me. I never had a stuffed animal in my life, but that wasn't the real reason I took it. The real reason was because I wanted something else of yours. I say *something else* because I already had your mustard-seed necklace. It fell off at the creek yesterday, as you were beating on me, and I picked it up and stuck it in my pocket when you turned away. Now you can hate me, Silver Nickles, if you don't already.

Everybody has always hated me, everywhere I ever lived. Either they make fun of my face or they make fun of my hair or they make fun of my glasses. (By the way, don't worry about buying new ones. I didn't tell Mother how they got broken.) Sometimes they even make fun of the way I laugh or the way I walk or the way I talk, as if *they're* perfect or something. That's why I like you so much, Silver Nickles. You're the only kid I ever knew who doesn't make fun of me all the time.

I have something else bad to tell you. I lied to you about having a father. I don't have a father. I never had a father, not one that I know about anyway. I started lying about it in first grade, when I realized that everybody else had a dad, but I didn't.

I know it was wrong to take your necklace and your dog, but my idea was to have something of you to keep, just in case we ever move again. But then last night I had a bad dream about how you were crying for your things. When I woke up, I remembered you telling me one time that you had only three things left of your parents: the necklace and the green dress and the stuffed dog they gave you when you turned two. Well, I couldn't take two of those things away, Silver, so I decided that if we ever move again, I'll just take my memories of you to keep. My memories of the parade and the water battle and sitting next to you in church. My memories of your funny jokes and of your determination to get a dog and of the way your eyes shine when you laugh. My memories of you cleaning out the kennels and putting up with my mother's meanness just to earn a little bit of money. My memories of your faith and your kindness. Those are the things I'll keep.

So here's your stuff, Silver Nickles. I took it to Rose's house this morning and she told me you were at the hospital, so I just brought it on in while you were gone. Hope you're not too mad, but I wouldn't blame you if you never talked to me again.

Your friend (I hope)????
Dudley Baxter

I carefully folded the paper and stuck it back in Woof-Woof's mouth, and then unclasped the mustard seed and fastened it around my neck. I finally felt whole again, feeling the weight of Woof-Woof on my legs and the mustard seed on my chest.

"Papaw," I called, "I found Woof-Woof and my necklace."

Papaw didn't answer.

I stood up and stripped out of Rose's clothes, and then pulled on some cutoffs and a T-shirt. There. Now I felt like myself: Silver Iris Nickles.

"Papaw," I yelled again. "I found Woof-Woof. I found my mustard seed."

"Good," Papaw answered from the other room. "Less money for me to spend. Get ready, Silver. We're heading to Swampville, to fetch you some new clodhoppers and a gown."

"A gown?" I asked, seeing the sun start to shine from behind the stained glass. The storm was over.

"For the wedding," Papaw called. "Miss Clara and I are getting hitched on Independence Day."

Independence Day? That was the Fourth of July . . . less than a month away. Papaw sure was in a hurry since his heart attack.

"Papaw," I said, balling up Rose's prissy white bedroom curtain and tossing it on my bed, "do we have to go shopping *today?* You just got home from the *hospital.*"

"You need shoes, don't you?" Papaw's voice and then his body, still dressed in the old soldier's uniform, floated into my room.

Two Dried-Up Old Lovebirds

I WAS WEARING YELLOW, lemony-yellow, with white patent-leather pumps. Papaw picked out the pumps, along with a new pair of sneakers, and I chose the gown. It was swishy and long and shiny, liquid sunlight, with a low scoop of a neckline and spaghetti straps. I had on my mustard seed with it, and the new nylon stockings Papaw bought in Swampville. Papaw got so mortified every time he had to buy me anything underwearlike that I thought he'd pass out from embarrassment. Buying bras really put him in a tizzy, and I needed a *strapless* one for the wedding. That really shook him up, having to stand at the counter at Kmart, shelling out his hard-earned cash for a bra that didn't even have straps *or* a blue flower. I refused to wear any more bras with flowers in the middle.

Standing under the trees with Papaw, Clara Cough Cough Cooper kept whipping out a pink powder puff from her pink purse, flouring her pink face with the stuff. Decked out in pink from the hat on her head to the shoes on her feet, she reeked of flowery perfume and hair spray. I swear, that lady was Rose Roberts in about another hundred years.

Papaw was wearing a white suit with a pink bow tie and a carnation. Papaw, in pink! I never thought I'd see the day. The sight of him there, his hair all slicked down and his face just glowing with happiness, almost made me cry. He'd gained back the weight he lost in the hospital, and then some.

"Are you going on a honeymoon, Mr. Bills?" Rose asked, fussing with her hair as we waited for Pastor Pete. I reckoned she was all worked up about the Miss Independence Contest that was taking place later in Swampville.

"Nah," Papaw said, "every day for the rest of our lives will be a honeymoon."

I rolled my eyes. "Clara," I said, picking at my nails, "did Papaw ever tell you about how he had pink toenails for Easter?"

Clara Cough Cough and Papaw ignored me, as they were smooching each other on their wrinkled old cheeks. Two dried-up old lovebirds, making out in the trees. How sick.

I sat on the grass and kicked off my shoes, making myself at least a little bit comfortable until Pastor Pete showed up.

"Silver!" said Rose. "You'll get your gown all grass-stained."

I shrugged. "Green goes good with yellow," I said, twirling my mustard seed.

Rose towered over me, a preening princess in pink. "Well," she said, looking at her satin-banded watch, "the Miss Independence Contest starts in less than an hour. Pastor Pete had better hurry."

"What did you write for your entry?" I asked. The girls were supposedly judged on four things: appearance, personality, how they answer a question from the judge on stage, and the 100-word essay entry titled "Why Am I Miss Independence?" I figured Rose probably wrote something about how she *has* to be Miss Independence because her parents leave her alone so much.

"What I wrote on the entry," Rose said, smirking, "is for me to know and you to find out." Her dreamcatchers glinted in the sunlight as I looked up at her.

"Here comes the pastor," rasped Clara, her pink lips smiling away. Pastor Pete was zooming through the middle of the park as if he'd been shot from a cannon, wearing a white shirt with black pants. He looked like a waiter, balancing a Bible instead of a tray.

I stood, smoothing out my gown, and took a deep breath. In about five minutes, Papaw would have a wife. And I'd have a grandmother, sort of. No way would I call her Mamaw, though. Clara would just have to do.

"Brother Walt! Sister Clara!" Pastor Pete burst into the middle of our little group, a man sent straight from Heaven to pronounce Papaw and Clara man and wife. I sighed, wishing with all my heart that Mama and Daddy and Emmie were here to see all this.

Pastor Pete stood against the bark of a tree, facing Papaw and Clara and Rose and me. He said some stuff about the miracle of marriage and then looked Papaw straight in the eye.

"Brother Walt," he said, serious as all get-out, "do you take this woman to be your lawful wedded wife?" Then he said all that stuff about in sickness and in health, for richer or for poorer, for better or for worse. I hoped Clara Cough Cough realized that Papaw could be a whole heck of a lot worse than he was today.

"I do," Papaw said and belched. I swear, you could dress the man up but you just couldn't take him anywhere.

"Sister Clara," Pastor Pete said, stifling a laugh, "do you take this man to be your lawful wedded husband?"

"I do," she said. Really it was "I" (cough, cough) "do" (cough, cough, cough, cough, kiss).

I looked away as they were kissing and saw a whole bunch of folks across the park, holding greyhound dogs on leashes. Gathering of the Greyhounds, said a banner tied between two trees and flapping in the breeze. Over to the right of the greyhounds was the stage, where the Miss Independence Contest would take place. I could see Rose from the corner of my eye, fidgeting, in a hurry to get over there.

Papaw and Clara Cough Cough Bills were doing the wedding rings, sliding them onto each other's fingers. I figured that putting a ring on Miss Clara would feel like banding a bird. Finally, it was over. Papaw and Clara kissed again, and again and again, standing like statues under the trees and not even moving when a pile of bird doo-doo plopped down behind them. I looked up and saw a cardinal, flashing red in the tree. As I watched, it flew, heading for the trees above the greyhound dogs.

And then I saw him. The Dud, standing halfway between the dogs and the stage, looking for all the world like he didn't know which way to go.

24

Scrawny-Looking Critters

"HEY, SILVER NICKLES." The Dud didn't look half-bad. His skin had cleared up, and he had a new haircut, short and spiky.

"Hey, Dud." I stared at him. Something else was different: his eyes! I could see the Dud's eyes, bright and jelly-bean green in the sunlight, with no dents on either side of the Dud's nose from the weight of those goofy black glasses. "Did you get contact lenses?" I asked, fiddling with my mustard seed.

The Dud nodded, fanning himself with some papers. We looked at each other for a minute.

"Are you mad at me?" asked the Dud.

I shook my head.

"You look nice in yellow," said the Dud.

I could actually feel myself blushing, and

looked away, over at the greyhound dogs.

"I picked up some papers for you," said the Dud, shoving the papers into my hand, "all about the adoption of retired greyhound racing dogs."

"Adoption?" I asked, riffling through the pages.

The Dud nodded. "When the dogs get too old or too slow to race, they're either put to death or adopted. I figured that would be something you'd be interested in."

"They're put to death?" I was horrified. "Just because they're too slow or old?" I took a few steps closer to the dogs, the Dud tagging along.

"Haven't you been reading about the plight of the greyhounds?" the Dud asked. "It's been all over the newspapers lately. Where have you been, Silver Nickles?"

I ignored him, moving toward the dogs.

"They're often left without water, starved, abandoned, or destroyed outright, just because they no longer measure up to somebody's expectations," said the Dud, sounding like the television reporter from the Channel 8 evening news. "Forty to sixty thousand of them are killed every year—killed or abandoned or sold to research laboratories."

"That's horrible!" I said, gawking at the greyhounds. They were so thin and delicate, scrawny-looking critters of skin and bone and big, sad eyes.

The Dud nodded. "That's why animal protection groups are working to make sure that more of them are adopted," he said. "Greyhound racing is one of the most popular spectator sports in the United States, so there are lots of the dogs being born all the time. Only problem is, they race for less than five years before retiring."

Tears filled my eyes. "And then they die," I said softly.

The Dud nodded, shuffling along through the grass toward the Gathering of the Greyhounds. "Come on," he said. "Come see them."

I trailed along, stopping at a blond-haired lady sitting on the ground and patting one of the dogs.

"Is this your dog?" I asked.

The lady smiled, nodding. "Her name is Delilah," she said. "Used to be Dashing Delilah Dazzler, back in her racing days. When she couldn't race so fast, she became mine. Now she's just Delilah, just plain old Delilah. She doesn't have to dazzle anybody anymore, do you, honey?" The lady stroked the dog's long nose. "She used to wear a muzzle, a racing muzzle, but I use it as a planter now." She smiled again.

"Delilah," said the lady, "is an angel in a dog's body. So gentle, so kind, so calm and trusting. She's got the best soul of any dog I know."

I reached down and patted Delilah's head. She looked up at me with those big, sad eyes. "Hi, Delilah," I said.

"Greyhounds hold a real place in history," said the lady as the Dud moseyed up beside me. He patted Delilah. "They were kept by the pharaohs in ancient Egypt and are the oldest known breed of dogs. During the Middle Ages, owning a greyhound was the exclusive right of noble people like kings and queens."

Not the Queen, I thought. *She gets stuck with those tiny little toy poodles.*

"Greyhounds are even in the Bible," said the lady. "The Book of Proverbs."

"How do you adopt one?" I asked.

"It's easy," said the lady. "You fill out an application form, telling what kind of home and family you have, and the adoption agency finds a greyhound to match your needs."

"Does it cost anything?" I asked, my heart racing.

"Only a hundred dollars," the lady said. "And that covers the shots, the transportation, the examination, a wire crate, and a special collar to grip the neck gently and securely when walking the dog on a leash. And you must use a leash, because greyhounds can run about forty-seven miles per hour."

"Wow," said the Dud. "That's faster than your papaw's truck, Silver."

I grinned. "Where can I get an application?" I asked.

"There's one in the packet of papers," said the lady. "It takes about two or three weeks to get your dog."

My heart jumped like a pup. *Two or three weeks!* Just in time for my birthday. I couldn't wait to get on home and fill out that application.

"See you here next year," called the lady, waving as we walked off. "The Gathering of the Greyhounds is for adopted dogs and their families."

"Bye," I hollered, feeling part of the group already. "See you next year."

"Ssshhh," hissed the Dud, nudging me in the ribs. "They just called your name from the stage."

25

A Mixed-Up Mess of Emotions

"SILVER IRIS NICKLES."

My name blared over the loudspeakers and echoed across the park. "Silver Iris Nickles, please report to the stage."

The Dud's mouth gaped open, and he gawked as if the Lord himself had called me to center stage.

"You'd better get up there, Silver," he said, nudging me again. "Maybe there's an emergency."

I went cold all over. Maybe it was Papaw. Maybe marrying Clara Cough Cough had given him another heart attack, or a stroke or something. Shaking, I made my way to the stage, where girls were lined up like flowers in shades of summertime pink and blue and green.

Scanning the pinks, I searched for Rose's red hair and her dreamcatchers. Rose wasn't there.

The red-faced man holding the microphone had started announcing my name again, and I motioned to him from below. "I'm Silver," I said, when he finally stopped talking and looked down at me.

"Silver!" he shouted. "Where have you been?"

He wasn't using the microphone, but with a mouth like that, he really didn't need to.

"I was at a wedding," I said, scuffing my shoes in the grass. I couldn't wait to get home and take them off. "And then I was at the Gathering of the Greyhounds."

The crowd cracked up, as if I'd said something hilarious.

"She was at a *wedding!*" hollered Mister Big Mouth into the microphone. "And then she was at the Gathering of the *Greyhounds!* I wonder why they call 'em *grey*hounds, when there's hardly a *grey* hair in the bunch!" Mister Big Mouth guffawed right into the microphone, a sound like a sick laughing hyena.

"Well," I replied, looking Mister Big Mouth straight in his beady little eyes, "my name is Silver, but do you see silver on *my* head?"

The crowd cracked up again and then broke into applause like thunder.

"She's not only pretty, but she's *funny*, too!" blared Mister Big Mouth, reaching down and taking my elbow. "Come on up here, Miss Silver Iris Nickles." He pulled me toward the steps leading up to the stage.

I resisted, leaning back like an old cow being led from the pasture to the milking barn. "Why?" I asked, jerking my elbow away and holding it tight against my body.

"Well, you are registered for the Miss Independence Contest," said the man, holding a sheet of paper before his beady little eyes. "Silver Iris Nickles, age twelve, Boghill Road."

"What?" I barked.

"Entered by Miss Rose Roberts," read the man.

Rose! I'd kill her, I truly would. I buried my face in my hands, shaking my head.

"Oh, come on, shy Iris," said Mister Big Mouth, tapping his foot.

"It's *Silver*," I said. "*Silver* Iris Nickles." I glared up at the man and then took a deep breath, gathering my nerve. Muttering to myself, I stomped up the steps, clumping along in those prissy white pumps like a cow in a prom gown and heels.

I stepped up beside Mister Big Mouth, not knowing what to do with my hands. I sized up the crowd, looking for that traitor Rose. The renegade Rose Roberts, double-crossing deceiver that she was. I stood there fuming, crossing my arms and blowing strands of hair from my face, while hundreds of eyes gawked up at me. I hated being on stage. I hated wearing a gown and pumps. I hated standing there on display like a Barbie doll in a store window, while a bunch of nosy folks judged my looks and my personality and my independence. I even hated Rose Roberts at that moment.

"Why Am I Miss Independence?" read Mister Big Mouth, putting his arm around my shoulders, which hurt already from those darn spaghetti straps.

"I, Silver Iris Nickles, am Miss Independence because of my strength and my courage and my determination. I am Miss Independence because of my backbone and my bravery, my grits and my gut, my spunk and my stubbornness. I am Miss Independence because of my never-ending faith, my eternal hope, and my everlasting trust that everything really will be all right in my life. I am Miss Independence because of my belief that I can get anything I want in this life, with a lot of hard work and a good dose of bullheadedness. I am Miss Independence because I, and I alone, can do anything."

Mister Big Mouth lowered the paper, as the crowd clapped and I blushed. I would never have written something like that, not in a million years.

"And now for your question," bellowed Mister Big Mouth. "What is your heart's desire, the thing you want most in this life?"

I didn't even have to think. "A dog," I said. "A retired greyhound racing dog."

Mister Big Mouth leered and the crowd cheered, clapping and whistling and hooting and hollering. Most of the racket seemed to come from one spot, somewhere in the middle of the army of people, and I peered that way, shading my eyes from the setting sun. There they were: Papaw, Clara, the Dud, and Renegade Rose. Papaw and Clara were holding hands, the Dud had a honking expression on his face, and Rose was practically jumping up and down. "Sil-ver, Sil-ver, Sil-ver," they all chanted. I was mortified and mad, a mixed-up mess of emotions in a yellow dress and white shoes.

"Let's hear it for Silver Iris Nickles," yipped Mister Big Mouth, as if I wasn't embarrassed enough already.

I sunk back into the line of girls, almost passing out from humiliation. No longer would Rose Roberts be my bosom buddy, not even if I grew a bosom as big as all get-out. Never.

I stood there in a haze, shaking, trying not to look at the crowd. I looked at the sky, I looked at my feet, I looked at Muckwater Mountain off in the distance. I looked at the contestants for Miss Independence as they swayed one by one up to the microphone, all full of big-haired beauty and big-eyed answers to Mister Big Mouth's questions. They all wore makeup, they all wore hair spray, and they all reeked of perfume and conceit. I thought that if their heads swelled any more, they'd just puff right up and float off the stage and into the sky, their fancy gowns all puffed out like parachutes.

Finally, it was over. Mister Big Mouth was ready to announce Miss Independence, and I was ready to strangle Rose Roberts. Forever was nothing compared to the time I'd spent standing on that stage, waiting for the end of this fiasco.

"And the winner is . . ." Mister Big Mouth whipped out a paper and held it before his eyes.

From behind the stage, the Swampville Elementary School band began to play "The

Star-Spangled Banner." I was starting to wonder if that was the only song they knew. A lady waited by the side of the stage, holding a glittery crown of red, white, and blue spangles.

"Miss Independence is . . ." Mister Big Mouth smirked, dragging out the suspense. It didn't bother me, but the other girls seemed to all be holding their breath and puffing out their chests. Now that I was finally relaxed, *they* were all nervous and uptight, breaking out in cold sweats all over their made-up faces. I sneaked a peek at my rooting section—Papaw and Clara and the Dud and Rose. They all seemed to be praying, with their hands clasped and eyes squeezed shut. I snickered, knowing something they didn't: I didn't have a snowball's chance in July. No way.

"A young lady of self-reliance and determination, beauty and brains, self-assurance and dedication . . . Miss Independence . . . Silver Iris Nickles!"

It was then that I fainted, out cold on center stage as the first fireworks exploded in the sky.

Something Truly Heavenlike

It WAS DARKER THAN THE DARK between the stars, and I lay flat on my back in bed . . . waiting.

Sure enough, it started: Papaw's snoring, snuffling and snarkling, and sawing logs, with a cussword cutting in every now and then, and then Clara's cough, all coming from the direction of the brand-new, double-wide bed Papaw had bought.

"They sure are noisy," I said to Blue Two, who wagged her tail in reply.

It was my birthday. At exactly 6:13, I'd turned thirteen. I'd been a teenager for about five hours now, and a dog owner for five days.

Blue Two had arrived early on Wednesday

morning, along with the adoption papers, a crate, a special leather collar, bright red leash, and her old racing muzzle from the days when she was Speedy Sarah Sizzler. Now that she wasn't so speedy anymore, she was just plain old Blue Two. And she was mine.

There wasn't a spot of blue on Blue Two, not one. She was brindled brown, with black stripes and four white paws that clicked quietly around Bark Shanty. Blue Two put me in mind of a deer, so tall and gentle and graceful, with big brown eyes brimming over with sweetness and obedience. I fell in love with her the minute I saw her.

And Blue Two loved me, too. She followed me around like a shadow, eating at my feet and sleeping in my bed. I even took her in the bathtub with me yesterday and used half a bottle of that high-priced dog shampoo I bought. I also bought a brush and a ball, and a big, blue bowl, which I put beneath the kitchen table.

Blue Two loved Bark Shanty, you could just tell. She loved my bed, and she loved the booger-green sofa, and she loved sleeping in the sunlight that streamed through the kitchen window. She loved running through the yard and sitting by the garden and taking long, slow walks through the swampland behind Bark Shanty. She loved playing catch in the woods and drinking cold water from the creek and batting at frogs with her paws.

It made me feel good, giving a home to Blue Two when she needed one, just like Papaw had done for me. I reckoned Bark Shanty and Muckwater Mountain were Hound Heaven to Blue Two.

Lying there on the night of my birthday and hugging Blue Two, I thought of how lucky I was. I really was grateful for what I had: a roof over my head and a bed to sleep in and food on the table. I was grateful for Papaw, and I was grateful for Blue Two, and I was even a little bit grateful for Clara, who made the best flapjacks on Muckwater Mountain.

There were still lots of things I *didn't* have, like a lot of clothes or a canopy bed or a boyfriend. But most of the things I didn't have, I didn't want anyway.

I clicked on Papaw's old flashlight and beamed it at the ceiling. There was Cleopatra and Johann Sebastian Bach and Elvis. There was Herbert Hoover and Harry Houdini and Hemingway. There was Plato and Pearly,

Sparkles and Spot, King and Queen, and Princess and Prince.

There were now sixty-eight dogs stuck on the ceiling, and one Dream Dog snuggled up in bed beside me. Blue Two was about as tall as I was, all stretched out across the sheet.

Sliding the circle of brightness slowly back and forth, up and down and all around, I shed light on each dog. Holding the flashlight like a holy white candle in my hands, I recited their names, as Blue Two thumped away with her long flyswatter of a tail.

"Rufus and Rex and Romeo," I whispered. "Sargent and Sancho and Snowy.

"Take a good look at the Dream Dogs," I said to Blue Two, "because tomorrow they're coming down."

I had lots of plans for tomorrow. I planned on baking that rhubarb pie I'd promised the Lord, ripping down the Dream Dog Display, and then making a scarecrow for our garden, which I'd been working at bringing back to par.

Clara said that I could use one of her old pink dresses for the scarecrow, and I figured *that* would scare off the critters as good as anything.

I beamed the flashlight toward my desk, illuminating the dreamcatcher necklace Rose gave me for my birthday, my mustard seed, Woof-Woof, the glittery crown I wore as Miss Independence, and Blue Two's old racing muzzle.

I closed my eyes, feeling Blue Two warm against my face. "Now I lay me down to sleep," I whispered. "I really love this dog a heap. And since you sent her by July, I owe you, Lord, a rhubarb pie."

I smiled and clicked off the flashlight, hearing Blue Two breathing in rhythm to Papaw's snores and Clara's coughs. "A-men," I whispered.

Staring at the stained-glass window and Blue Two's silhouette dark against the light of the night, I saw the moon, sliding from behind a cloud. It was big and bright and happy, the happiest moon I'd seen in a long, long time.

Moving my head from the pillow to Blue Two's warm body, I could hear the beating of her heart and knew without a doubt that something truly heavenlike had happened. All because of faith that could move Muckwater Mountain, and a lot of hard work, and a little bit of luck.

Smiling, I stashed the flashlight beneath my pillow and closed my eyes, falling fast asleep.